The Kabalevs'

Chapter Or

I keep a diary, meticulously.
Without it I would lose track of r. .
I have no doubt I would also forget any dream ..
nights might visit upon me.
Without a diary I might not even be able to tell them apart.

It was Christmas Day 1979.
A white Christmas.
Crisp, fresh snow had settled on the side-walk.
I had been walking my black Labrador, Duffy, for half an
hour, and now we were heading back to my mother's
home, River House.
I had to tread carefully, while walking Duffy home,
because I might easily slip.
My flimsy shoes weren't made for this weather and Duffy
wasn't an easy dog to walk in these conditions.
He was eager to explore the wood, trying to pull me into it,
and I had to drag him back.
I remembered how my father had given me the dog back in
1967, when I was still a small child.
Duffy had been in my life ever since.
Jim Watson, my father, had long ago disappeared.
He had divorced my mother and then vanished into
oblivion.
I wondered what he might be doing now.
My mother had recovered quickly from the divorce, as
many women seem to.
She had soon remarried.
My mother's new husband, my new stepfather, was a
handsome submariner.

Like a lot submariners he had a nickname.

Riff.

Duffy and I were heading back to their new marital home now.

I could see it, there by the river and opposite the deep wood.

Duffy was even more eager to explore the wood now, but I restrained him.

We crossed the road, just opposite the neighbour's place, and headed for the house.

Back in the summer of 1976, when my mother married Riff, he had whisked her away to his own country, Canada,.

She had taken Duffy with her.

I stayed in England, with no mother and a vanished father, which wasn't so bad really.

I missed Duffy though.

For three years I struggled along, fending for myself, trying to piece my life back together again as best I could, after all that had happened.

Then, six months ago and out of the blue, I received a letter.

The letter was from my mother, and contained a plane ticket, and instructions on how to become a fledgeling Canadian citizen.

To cut a long story short, this was how I came to be here, in Canada, on a beautiful Christmas morning, walking Duffy.

My mother and Riff owned other dogs, but Duffy was mine.

Dogs are clever animals.

Though I'd been out of his sight, sound, and scent, (for over three years), Duffy had never forgotten me.

And of course I had never forgotten Duffy.

We were at the front door of the house and let ourselves in. There was a mad rush of other dogs, who were frantically sniffing Duffy to see where he'd been.

Duffy stood there patiently as the other dogs tried to get a clue to his adventure by smelling his private parts.

Annabel, the huge white Pyrennian Mountain dog, was twice the size of Duffy, but Duffy was the boss.

The two smaller dogs, (Nemo and Henry), were little sweethearts.

They all took turns circling and then sniffing Duffy.

I took off Duffy's leash and joined Riff in the living room. There was a wonderful smell of roasting meat mixed with pine, from the tree.

"Here you are Charlie" Riff said, handing me a glass of something.

It was scotch.

He raised his glass, and I raised mine to him.

"Bette asked us all to go to the service before lunch. Are you all right with that?" he asked me.

Bette was Riff's mother, but he called her Bette, just like everyone else, (although not to her face; then he called her 'mother').

"Sure" I answered.

I wasn't really a religious person.

I'd had the usual Sunday School education, and Religious Studies at school, but I wasn't sure I believed in a God.

It must be very comforting to believe in a God, I thought.

"Then Bette's going to join us for lunch" he informed me.

This was great news.

I really liked Bette.

She hardly knew me, really, but she had already started to refer to me as her grandson.

Riff was Bette's only child and my mother was Riff's only wife.

It was unlikely that Bette would have any grandchildren apart from me.

I could hear my mother's voice from the kitchen.

"I don't want you plying Charlie with drink Riff" she was saying without humour. "He gets aggressive!"

Riff raised an eyebrow and silently mouthed the words "Do you?"

I shook my head, and Riff chuckled.

The dogs had finished sniffing and were restlessly circling the open plan living space.

The smell of the meat promised a feast and they were impatient for it.

"We don't stand on ceremony in this house Charlie, I think you know that by now" Riff said as he headed for the Christmas tree.

"But usually we wait till after dinner before we hand the presents out".

He handed me a box wrapped in green.

"It's just that I thought you'd appreciate this now. I don't want you to wait".

I took the box, held it, not wanting to unwrap it for fear of incurring my mother's wrath.

"Open it" he insisted, with a fierce smile.

I read the gift tag and unwrapped the gift.

It was a beautiful pair of black winter boots.

This was exactly what I needed.

The shoes I was wearing, my only pair of shoes in fact, were made for summer, and they were about two years old.

"Thank you so much Riff" I said.

I didn't know if I should hug him, shake him by the hand, or what.

My relationship hadn't quite settled into its proper place yet.

He was my stepfather, but he wasn't quite old enough to be my father.

He was more like an older brother in some ways.

"Try them on" he ordered.

Without hesitation I slipped them on.

They were a perfect fit.

I walked about in them.

Duffy came over to sniff them.

"These are MY special gift to you Charlie. I noticed you needed a pair" he explained.

My mother was out of the kitchen now, and in the living room.

She spied the boots.

"Oh I see you found the boots I bought you" she said, and there were layers of poison in her tone.

My mother had nothing to do with the boots, of that I was sure.

It didn't stop her from wanting the credit for them, though.

Riff, I knew, had chosen, bought and wrapped this gift to me.

Even the gift tag said 'Happy Xmas, Best Wishes, Riff'.

Riff might not be able to handle my mother, but I had years of experience.

I strode over to my mother and hugged her warmly.

"Oh mum" I gushed. "These are just what I needed. Thank you. It's too much".

She put her poison away temporarily.

"I hoped you might like them, but I was going to wait till AFTER dinner".

She shot Riff a look that was designed to freeze him to his core.

"I couldn't let him go off to Bette's service wearing those old things" Riff recovered, pointing briefly at my down-at-heel shoes, still on the carpet.

"Perhaps you're right" she agreed.

"Talking of which; I think we should get ready soon" Riff suggested.

My mother spent the next half an hour getting ready for church, and Riff was becoming more agitated.

He kept glancing at his watch but said nothing.

He couldn't hold it any longer.

"We'll be late Dianne if you don't get your skates on".

His tone was as light as he could make it.

It would have been better if he'd said nothing.

"YOU can go to your mother's service stinking of booze and looking like a tramp if you wish" she said. "I have a bit more class than that!"

She was ready in another five minutes, but I was under the impression that she was dragging her heels deliberately, as Riff's punishment for trying to speed her up.

We drove for fifteen minutes along snowy roads until we arrived at the white wooden church.

The service had already started, and had probably been in progress for five minutes.

I wondered, if Riff had said nothing, (instead of "We'll be late Dianne if you don't get your skates on"), I was sure we'd have been here on time.

We crept in as quietly as we could hoping no one would notice.

Bette noticed.

She was in in the middle of her greeting to her congregation.
She was dressed in blue with a white dog collar.
She was red-cheeked with hair as white as a cloud.
She introduced the first hymn; In The Cold Midwinter.
The frail and ancient organist began to play and the congregation joined in after a few bars introduction.
The hymn ended and Bette began her sermon.

"Christmas is a tradition that goes back many thousands of years. We like to think that it dates back to the birth of Jesus, but it's even more ancient than that. Is it a coincidence that the Winter Solstice is only just passed? There is an ancient ruin in Ireland, five thousand years old. On the Winter Solstice, and at no other time of the year, the sun rises and its light beams through the doorway, illuminating the inner sanctum almost as if by magic. This ancient place is called Newgrange. If ever you visit the Emerald Isle I urge you to visit it. In a way It's quite like the manger you'd imagine Jesus was born in. I'm not for a minute suggesting that Our Lord was born in Ireland. An Irishman once told me that Jesus could never have been born in Ireland. I asked him why that was. He answered me, because they couldn't find three wise men or a virgin".
There was a suppressed chuckle, but a frosty silence from some quarters.
"What I AM suggesting is that Jesus's message isn't especially powerful at THIS time of year. His message is equally powerful regardless of his supposed birthday. The Solstice though! THAT is magical. It's the beginning of Winter, and pagans would bring living trees into their homes, believing that, by doing so, they might encourage new life in the face of death. It's called 'sympathetic

magic'. Believe something and it WILL be true. This brings me back now to the message that Jesus brought us. There IS a life everlasting. Love one another. Not one day a year! Every single day of the year. I want you to believe this. If you believe it with all your heart then it WILL be true!"

She announced the next hymn.

Away in a manger.

The service lasted about a half an hour.

I'm sure Bette would have been happy to make the service longer but she knew that turkeys were cooking in every household.

Then Bette was at the church door, shaking the hand of every parishioner.

She smiled at each of them, giving them all an individual and pertinent message of good cheer.

Finally she came to greet her son, his wife, and me.

"So sorry we were a bit late" Riff apologised.

"Oh I know" said Bette, still smiling."These roads are treacherous. At least you made it safely. How are you Dianne? And how's my favourite grandson?"

I loved it when she called me this. I couldn't help smiling. She had reserved a special smile for me which she now allowed to shine.

My mother's smile didn't reach her wide eyes.

"We should hurry back or the turkey will be ruined" my mother said.

"Yes, we can't have that, can we Charlie?" Bette said.

We were soon back at River House.

My mother had taken to calling the marital home River House, because it was right beside the river.

This made it sound a lot grander than it really was.

Dinner was served.

"This is your first Christmas here Charlie. How do you like it?" Bette asked.

"I love it Bette. You're guaranteed a white Christmas!" I answered.

"That's true" she agreed.

"Will you say Grace mother?" Riff was asking Bette.

"Certainly" she said.

We all held hands around the table.

"Thank you Lord on this special day. The day that you gave your Son to us. We ask you to bless this food. Bless all those who sit around this table", she gave my hand a little squeeze, "and let us never forget the hungry and lonely, who are always in our thoughts but especially so today. Amen".

We all repeated 'Amen'.

Riff was at the head of the table carving, the turkey.

It smelled delicious, and we all said as much.

Before long Bette was saying that she was worried about her organist.

"He's going blind, so it won't be long before he can't read a single note in his hymn book. But I'm more worried that he's simply too ill to play any more" she explained.

"Why not ask Charlie?" said Riff.

"Oh Charlie" Bette said to me. "Do you think it's something you'd be able to do? No that's a silly question; of course you're ABLE! Is it something that you would WANT to do?"

"Sure" I said. "Why not?"

"I'd be able to pay you a small amount every month. Not very much, but a hundred dollars a month" she offered.

To be honest I was in desperate need of money.

I was trying and failing to be self-supporting.

I had to find rent every month.

I had to live too.

It was all too much.

An extra hundred dollars would make all the difference.

I accepted.

I would start just as soon as Bette was able to talk to her current organist.

Soon it was time to open presents.

I'd bought presents that were within my meagre budget.

I'd bought Riff pipe tobacco.

I'd bought Bette some perfume.

I'd bought my mother a silver necklace.

My mother said nothing as she put it on.

"How pretty" Bette said. "Oh Dianne it suits you so well."

My snorted my mother derisively.

"It's a bit plain Charlie" she said.

I told her I'd kept the receipt so she could choose something else if she wanted.

I could see that my mother had decided already.

The necklace was so cheap anyway that a refund was more trouble than it was worth.

Bette gave me thick socks to wear with my new boots, and a pair of fingerless gloves.

I wasn't expecting a present from my mother. She'd already claimed that she'd bought my boots.

Nevertheless she handed me a gift.

I unwrapped it. It was a shirt.

There was no doubt in my mind that the shirt came from a charity shop.

It had a hideous design of pink and purple, like a very bad acid trip.

I thanked her profusely.

Thankfully no one in the room was screaming at me to try it on.

I never wore it.

I kept the shirt for about a year in case my mother asked about it.

She never asked about it.

Riff was fingering his beard, looking thoughtful.

"I was just wondering about our next door neighbour, Mrs Van Nord" he said.

He explained to his mother.

"She's a lovely old lady. A piano teacher, actually," he said to me. Then, to his mother, he continued, "I have a feeling she's been spending the day all alone".

"Well we can't have that, can we?" Bette said brightly.

My mother's lips became a thin line.

My mother was not the kind of woman to have her hostessing skills questioned.

Bette was overstepping an invisible boundary here, though she didn't know it.

"I will see to Mrs Van Nord" my mother spat gruffly.

She went to her kitchen and made up a plate from the leftover food, of which there was plenty.

"I just thought she might need a bit of company, today of all days! We could invite her over here!" Riff said, trying to smooth any ripples he might have caused.

"Mrs Van Nord is a proud woman, Riff. She wouldn't want us to pity her" said my mother, as if to a child.

She stormed out of the house, carrying a plate of Christmas dinner, and slammed the front door behind her.

This woke up the dogs, who had been lazing in front of the open fire. Once awake they remembered there might be food, and ran about in the hope we might feed them.

The three of us were left in a stunned silence.

We were all far too polite to comment on my mother's behaviour.

I don't want to paint a picture of my mother as being nasty or evil.

She just looks at the world as if it's HER doll's house, and all the people in it are HER dolls.

I really think it's as simple as that.

I slept over that night, with Duffy on my bed, stroking his fur as I fell asleep..

The next day Riff offered to drive me back to my apartment in town.

I gladly accepted the ride.

"I wish I was in a better position to help you out with your finances" Riff said.

I knew that his wage would be fully stretched as long as he lived with my mother. She wanted the best of everything, and she always got it.

I told him I understood.

He dropped me off outside Reds Bar.

I lived directly above it.

I thanked him and he drove away.

"Hey" said Roger in greeting.

Roger was one of my flatmates.

He was the same age as me.

He had dark curly hair where mine was fair and straight.

His eyes as brown as mine are blue.

We were both studying music at the local university.

He was smoking a joint of home-grown weed.

"Hey Roger" I returned his greeting, and he handed me the joint.

"How was your Christmas?" he asked.

"Fine" I said. "How about yours?!

"Couldn't wait to get back home" he answered.

"Me too" I laughed.

"That bad huh?"

I put a record on the stereo.

The fifth Brandenburg Concerto.

Bach filled the room.

"Fancy a beer?" I asked him.

"Sure" he said. "Downstairs? Reds?"

"Yeah" I said. "I want to celebrate. My grandmother just gave me a gig!"

I told him all about it.

"Wow! You, in a church, every Sunday! What about the fire hazard?"

"What do you mean?"

"Aren't you worried you might burst into flames crossing the threshold?"

"I never tire of your witty banter, old chum" I said in my best Noel Coward.

I freshened up and we headed down to our favourite bar, Reds.

"You know" observed Roger "as long as we are alive we are never going to live as close to a bar again".

"Let's make the most of it then".

Less than a minute later we had ordered a jug of beer.

The place wasn't exactly packed but there was still a great atmosphere.

A young woman came over to us.

"Hi Barb" said Roger.

"Hi Roger, Charlie. Happy Christmas" she said.

Barb was another of my flatmates.

"Where's Mark?" I asked her.

She pointed.

"How was your Christmas?" I asked her.

"Bit of a damp squid" she said.

"Don't you mean squib?" Roger corrected.

"What the fuck is a squib?" she asked. "That's made up. You just made that up!"

Roger was having a giggling fit now, and nothing could stop him.

"I was trying to be nice, and invite you to join us" she said. "I can see now I shouldn't have bothered".

She wasn't angry. This was all just part of our chemistry.

Roger picked up our jug of beer and we joined Mark and Barb at their table.

Before long we were joined by another couple; Ursula and Mick.

These two were the last of my flatmates.

It was the same story for all six of us.

We'd spent Christmas Day with our various families, but it was all too much for us, and we had to head home to safety.

Barb worked as a waitress at a fish restaurant, called the Fisherman's Rest.

"Are you looking for a job?" Barb was asking me.

"Depends" I said.

"The Fisherman's is looking for a part time waiter".

The money wouldn't be great, but tips could be good.

I'd never waited tables before, but I was sure it couldn't be that difficult.

I told her I was happy to give it a go.

"You'll be fine. There's nothing to it" she told me.

She promised me that she'd arrange an interview in the next couple of days.

Barb had waited tables in other restaurants too.

One of these restaurants was called Harold's House, an up-market steak house.

The cellar-man there, Rob, had become her firm friend.
"You'd like him" she said.
She described him; red-headed, burly and bearded.
Apparently he possessed a wicked sense of humour.
Barb told me that Rob was gay, and had been in a
relationship for the last five years.
By now I was understandably intrigued.
Ursula had been whispering to Mick, and Mick was
nodding
"Ursie suggested we throw a New Years Eve party" Mick
announced.
"Great idea Ursie" exclaimed Barb. "I'll invite Rob", she
nudged me and she gave me a smile.

It was New Years Eve 1979.
A Tuesday.
I'd already started work at the Fisherman's.
It was only two evenings a week but I wasn't about to
complain.
I thought I might manage to survive quite well just on my
tips.
By pay-day I would be able to cover my rent.
Things were beginning to look good.
I had every hope that this was going to be a great New
Year.
Our New Years Eve party was in full swing by ten o'clock.
I was talking some sort of nonsense with Roger, as we
usually did, when Barb opened our front door to a burly,
bearded red-head.
This was obviously Rob.
He was exactly as Barb had described.
She dragged Rob over to us, introduced us, then left us to
our own devices.

"I thought you might be coming with someone" I broke the ice as best I could.

He looked at me quizzically.

"Oh, you mean Al" he said, catching up with me. "He'll be here later."

In conversation it turned out that Harold's House was looking for a waiter.

Roger said that HE was looking for work.

He wasn't able to work full time though.

I said that I could use another part time job.

Al figured that the full-time job could be split between two part-time people.

He promised he'd sort us out with interviews before the week was out.

With all the business out of the way we could party!

Rob's partner turned up about an hour later.

He was as bearded and burly as Rob, but was black haired where Rob was red-headed.

"This is Al" said Rob.

Al's handshake was firm and warm, with strong fingers that gripped my hand sincerely.

We took to each other straight-away .

By midnight everyone was as merry as tradition dictated. Someone counted down from ten to zero and there was a cheer and spontaneous eruption of 'Auld Lang Syne'.

Whether by accident or design my last kiss of the seventies was with Al.

He kissed me far too passionately than he should have, considering he was in a relationship with someone.

My first kiss of the eighties, just a few seconds later, was with Rob.

The three of us had a big communal hug and were inseparable for the next hour or so as the party died away.

It was official.

1980 was going to be a great year.

I'd found two new friends, I had two part time jobs, and I had a church gig.

It was Thursday, January the tenth, 1980.

It was a freezing cold morning, and every breath turned to steam.

The pavement was iced over and snow had piled up high at the kerb.

I walked briskly in spite of the slippery ice, and this kept me warm.

My new boots were made for this kind of weather; warm fleece inside and with a good sole outside that gripped the ice.

My goal was soon in sight; the university building that housed the music department. It was nine o'clock as I entered the music department building, (known by a few people as the 'Robert Long').

The building must have been named after someone, (the builder or founder perhaps), but I never researched who Robert Long was.

Most simply referred to the building as "The Oblong", even though it was perfectly cube-shaped.

Once inside the Oblong, (where it was mercifully warm), I descended the stairwell into the basement where the rehearsal rooms were located.

At 9 o'clock on this particular morning the basement was empty and I had my choice of rooms, and of pianos.

I chose the room with the best piano. Of course.

Who wouldn't?

I chose the room with the Steinway grand piano in it and now I could practice for an hour before my piano lesson.

I sat at the piano and pulled out my sheet music.

I remember I was trying to perfect a Beethoven sonata, in D major. The first movement, (the Presto), pushed my technique to the limit but the slow movement could have been written for me.

I played the first and second movements for an hour, and then I was ready for my piano lesson with Miss Clokovsky.

Olivia Clokovsky was a very fierce-seeming woman with tight, iron coloured hair.

Everything about her seemed to symbolize economy, whether it was her trim figure or her terse use of language.

I knocked on her door and she responded with the word "Come".

I entered and she instructed me to "Be seated".

I sat at the piano and she sat neatly on a chaise longue at the other end of the room.

"I will hear the Beethoven", she said.

I opened my sonata book to the first movement of the D major.

"The slow movement" she clarified.

I turned a few more pages, to the D minor slow movement.

I took control of all my feelings and breathed deeply.

I began to play.

I had decided that the real trick to playing this particular movement was to choose the tempo carefully.

Too slow and all emotion would be drained from it. Too fast and the by the time you reached the coda it would be out of control.

One of the things I love about Beethoven is his use of light and shade. He can have you in the throes of dark passion and suddenly he pulls the very earth from under you, leaving you floating in air, threatening to hurtle you to your doom. In that moment of weightlessness he gently catches you and glides you down on angelic motifs. Then he has you caught up again in more dark passions which thrust you along to the end.

This slow movement is typical of Beethoven, and I felt so at one with it today.

I brought the piece toward the closing chords.

With very little drama I finished playing the final chord and lifted my hands from the keyboard.

I turned to Miss Clokovsky.

She had tears in her eyes.

"Forgive me" she said. "It is just that I have never heard this movement played so beautifully".

I was unused to Miss Clokovsky being so emotional.

She was usually very unforgiving, and could easily make me feel I was wasting my time in pursuit of musical excellence.

I found it difficult to accept her praise. It was so wonderful hearing her words, and yet still I disbelieved them.

She wiped her eyes and told me a story.

"I studied piano with a man called Felix Swinstead" She began.

I had heard of him.

I had learned to play some pieces he'd composed.

"Swinstead studied under Carl Czerny", she continued.

I had, of course, heard of Czerny.

"In turn, Czerny had studied under Beethoven" she said, looking at me to see my reaction.

I realized, that in a way, Miss Clokovsky was handing me a baton, or a torch.

She saw my expression and smiled.

"Exactly Mr Watson! You now know that you have a great responsibility!" She was very serious, or rather, more serious than usual. "I expect nothing less of you than excellence. Do you understand?"

I told her that I did.

She told me, then, that we should cut the lesson short.

She had nothing more to say on the matter.

I had mastered the Beethoven slow movement and talking about it would be a waste of energy.

Waste was not a concept Miss Clokovsky understood or tolerated.

I took advantage of her offer to cut the lesson short, and packed my sheet music back into my satchel.

"Next week" she told me "you will have prepared the Kabalevsky".

The Kabalevsky she was talking about is a sonata, technically demanding, quite long, and not easy to memorize.

Kabalevsky is the name of the composer.

Preparing the piece for the next lesson would be an impossible struggle.

Miss Clokovsky's assignments were the hardest of things to accomplish. This is why I had to practice three hours a day, every day.

I would practice for an hour at 9 o'clock, then at lunchtime, and then for another hour after all the lectures were done.

I knew that, even with twenty one hours a week of practice, it was unlikely I would be able to "have the Kabalevsky prepared".

Before starting university life I rarely practiced more than an hour a day.

Now, though, I needed to practice three hours a day, at least, just to keep up with Miss Clokovsky's demands.

The bell rang signifying the division of periods.
One lesson ended and another began.

My Theory teacher, (a man of great genius, called Doctor
Farnham), set an assignment for the class.
Each student, he said, had to write a chorale in the style of
Bach, correctly following the rules of counterpoint that we
were supposed to have learned.
(A chorale is a short piece of music to be sung by soprano,
alto, tenor and bass voices.)
We had a week to finish the chorale.
Doctor Farnham was almost twenty years older than me, a
handsome man, but intimidating and aloof.
Even so I found myself falling a little bit in love with him
and there can be no doubt it was because of his great
intellect.
Unfortunately for me, though, Doctor Farnham didn't seem
to know that I existed.
I decided that I would write a chorale the like of which had
never been heard before.
I decided that Doctor Farnham would notice me, even if
only a little bit, because my chorale would be so beautiful
and irresistible.
My Chorale was going to grab his attention!
(Bette had asked me if I could start playing organ in her
church this coming Sunday, and she had given me an old
hymn book of my own.)
I looked through the hymn book now, for words that I
could set to music.
I turned a page of the hymn book, and these words jumped
out at me.

Alas, and did my saviour bleed?

And did my sovereign die?
Would he devote his sacred head
For sinner such as I?

The first syllable would to be sung using a very tight C
minor chord and then, on the second syllable, the alto rose
a semitone from a G to an Ab.
It was instant drama.
It's almost impossible to describe music using only words.
It would be so much easier if I could just play you my
chorale, but since I can't play it we're left with only words.
My chorale was more than half finished now and I was
well pleased with the way it was going.

Tonight was my fifth night working at The Fisherman's
Rest.
I would be working there every Wednesday and Thursday
night, from seven till midnight.
The manager had shown me how to work the coffee
machine.
"Clean out the old grounds, then add a few scoops of fresh
coffee" he explained.
It seemed easy enough.
"Then add a pinch or two of salt".
I'd never heard of adding salt to coffee before.
"Why add salt?" I asked.
He looked at me as if I was mad.
"Because it tastes better" he said emphatically.
"Oh, I see" I said, but I didn't see at all.
Nevertheless he was the boss and I had to do his bidding.
Barb, my flat mate, had been instrumental in getting me
the job.

She covered for me while I learned the ropes, and until I picked up speed.

There was another waitress there called Lee Ping, a plump Chinese girl, full of energy.

Lee Ping asked me to get "fidderhair" from the kitchen.

I really wasn't sure what she meant, so she repeated "Fidderhair! Fidderhair!".

A little confused I made it into the kitchen and asked the chef "Lee Ping wants fidderheair.

"Fidderhair?" he echoed.

"Yes, fidderhair!"

"Oh" he began to chuckle. "Fiddleheads!"

He put a portion of fiddleheads on a serving dish, and handed it to me, still chuckling.

Barb came into the kitchen with some plates and cutlery.

"Table two, Charlie" she said.

I went out into the restaurant, gave Lee Ping her fiddleheads, and then attended to the couple at table two.

I took their order and offered them the wine list.

The man waved the wine list away with a hand.

"We'll have coffee" said the man, who was probably about forty and well dressed.

His companion was elegantly dressed in black, accessorized with silver necklace and matching earrings.

I saw that the coffee machine needed refilling.

I did as I had been instructed and put a few scoops of ground coffee into the paper filter, followed by a pinch or two of salt.

I took the fresh coffee to table two.

The well dressed man called me back to the table about a minute later.

"This coffee tastes salty" he said.

"Yes" I said, and I must have looked and sounded very matter-of-fact about it.

"There's salt in our coffee" he repeated.

"Yes" I said again.

The man was momentarily stumped.

"You put salt in our coffee?" he asked.

"Yes" I said again.

"Why would you put salt in our coffee?" he asked.

"Because it tastes better" I said, repeating what the manager had told me.

"I'd like to speak to the manager" he said restraining his anger.

A minute or two later the manager was at table two, talking to the well dressed man and his elegant companion. I waited at other tables while they talked, but I could see by the way their heads seemed to nod in my direction that I was the subject of their conversation.

The manager apologised to the couple and let them dine for free.

I didn't get a tip.

In fact I'd go so far as to say that, as they left, the couple gave me a look that suggested I was of limited intelligence. The manager came up to me, once the couple had left, and said "Don't put any more salt in the coffee machine".

I wasn't given the sack! That was a plus anyway

It was Friday the eleventh of January.

I practiced the Kabalevsky for an hour.

Then, at the bell, I made my way to my first lecture of the day; Theory with Doctor Farnham.

I loved his lectures.

He seemed to shine, star-like, as he explained to his students the rules of counterpoint.

I've heard it said that every person has one teacher they can say inspired them. Farnham was mine.

"Good morning boys and girls" he said, despite the fact that all his students were over the age of nineteen.
One of the students, Elizabeth Summer, was in her forties, which some of my peers thought was ancient.
"Today I want to quickly recap some of the more obscure rules of counterpoint. Remember, first of all, that these rules evolved over centuries, and that every single one of these rules is based on what our ears already know. For example," he went over to the piano.
"Parallel fourths and fifths sound like monks".
He played a string of six or seven chords.
"Can you hear?" he asked, and every head in the room gave a nod.
"And that is why they have to be avoided at all costs".
The students chuckled quietly.
Farnham was dark and brooding like the hero from a Regency novel.
The lecture continued, and every student was as enraptured as I was.
At the end of the lecture Farnham said,
"Don't forget I need your assignments handed in by next Thursday, at the latest".
My assignment was nearly ready, and as the bell went, (signifying the end of lecture), I went to the front of the classroom to show it to him.
The lecture room was emptying of all the other students now.
He didn't even look at me as he took the manuscript paper from me.

He took a pencil and marked the paper with a line across every chord, saying "parallel fourth, parallel fourth, parallel fourth, parallel fourth!"
he looked at me now.
"It needs a bit more work"
I felt embarrassed and sick.
I had just broken the very same rule he had been reinforcing.
I felt more humiliated in that moment than ever in my life before.
Humiliated though I was I still had something akin to pride.
Or was it simply stubbornness?
I wasn't going to crumble in front of this man whom I adored.
"Yes" I told him. "It needs more work."
He gave the paper one last look, then handed it back to me saying.
"You have until Thursday".

On the morning of Sunday the thirteenth there was the toot of a car horn outside the apartment.
It was a yellow Ford Cortina, and my mother was in the driving seat.
I had my hymn book and the Kabalevsky sheet music with me, together with an overnight bag.
I was going to make my début playing at Bette's church.
She started the car.
"I'm so relieved that Riff will be going away to sea soon, for the next six months" she was saying.
I made encouraging noises in the spaces she left.
"I'm sick and tired of being taken for granted by him and his mother."

I couldn't believe Bette would take anyone for granted.
I found it hard to believe Riff would take advantage either,
but I said nothing, just made the right noises.
"Do you know he beats me up? Oh yes, from the very first
day of our marriage! I had a black eye and a broken
tooth!"
I was certain that if she really HAD suffered such injuries
she wouldn't have waited over three years before telling
me. I didn't believe her, but still I made all the right noises.
I knew from experience that it would be useless to
contradict her anyway.
She was driving and giving me her monologue.
"You've never seen it Charlie, because I've shielded you
from it all, but he's dangerous".
She stressed the last word by raising the volume and pitch.
"I wish now that I'd never agreed to divorce your father.
He may have been an alcoholic but he was a good man and
I loved him. I never loved Riff. And besides, he needs a
splint to keep it up in the bedroom".
I felt uncomfortable thinking about my mother and Riff
doing anything in the bedroom, even if it involved a splint.
"Oh by the way" she said, changing the subject. "I've been
speaking to Mrs Van Nord next door. She's asked me to
get you to pop round to see her. I said you could visit her
after you've played organ."
I wondered what that could be about.
"I'm sure she'll tell you" my mother answered my question.

Bette wore grey, still with her white dog collar.
We hugged our hello and she talked me through the
service.
It all seemed straightforward enough.

"And will you be staying for Sunday dinner afterwards?" she asked.

"I'm afraid not Bette. I have to see Mrs Van Nord" I explained.

"Oh" she sighed. "Is that the piano teacher? Never mind. I'll see you next Sunday, and maybe you can stay for dinner then".

I promised.

It was time to meet Mrs Van Nord.

I rang her front door bell and she answered.

"You must be Charlie" she said. "Come in, come in".

She was about sixty, with Nordic features and colouring.

She had a very slight accent.

She smelled of lavender.

There was the steady ticking of a grandfather clock.

She had made a fresh pot of tea and offered me a cup.

"Now Charlie, I hear you are a very fine pianist" she said, and I couldn't tell if this was statement or question.

"I don't know about that" I said.

"Play something for me" she said.

I sat at her piano.

Resting on the piano was a picture frame containing a photo of a ruggedly handsome man.

I played a Brahms intermezzo, a favourite of mine.

"Beautiful" she said, clapping her hands in appreciation.

"Maybe you would be in a position to do me a very great favour" she said.

Then she told me that she was soon to go into hospital.

She wanted her students to continue with their lessons.

She asked me if I thought it would be possible to teach some of her best students in her stead.

I said that I could only manage it if I could teach them on a Saturday.

Mrs Van Nord thought that this could be arranged.

She would make a series of phone calls.

By the following Saturday, (the nineteenth of January), I would start to teach ten of Mrs Van Nord's best students.

It was Monday the fourteenth of January.

It was just after six in the evening.

I donned a clean white shirt, freshly ironed, then a black clip-on bow-tie.

I pulled on a pair of black trousers and my new black boots.

I put on my warm jacket because it was still freezing outside.

Then I walked on icy streets to Harold's House and began my duties as waiter, serving fine food and wine to the good and great who chose to dine there.

Though I had lived in this foreign city for the best part of a year I still retained a strong English accent.

It was this accent, I'm sure, that was the reason I passed the job interview.

It certainly wasn't anything to do with my waiting skills.

I had to learn those skills on the job; new skills, different to anything I might have learned at the Fisherman's.

For example, I had been taught, by the manager, to open a bottle of wine in a very particular way.

I was shown how to place a tea towel across my thigh and then, resting it on the tea towel, uncork the bottle.

On this night I waited at the table of a middle aged couple, most likely husband and wife celebrating an anniversary.

I took their order and offered them the wine list.

I remember they chose the house white wine, even though it didn't go with their steaks.

I went to the wine cellar and asked the cellar-man for the bottle of white.

Rob, of course, was the cellar-man.

Rob handed me the bottle of white, which was wet from being in the chiller, and I took it up to my diners.

I put the cloth across my thigh.

I rested the wet bottle on the cloth, as I'd been taught, and then took the corkscrew to it.

I always dreaded this part of the job.

I would much rather have put the bottle between my thighs to gain better purchase, but this would have looked slovenly.

I imagined that there would come a time when a bottle would slip off my thigh and then crash to the wooden floor.

I had the cork almost out of the bottle now and gave the corkscrew one final tug.

The corkscrew flew out of the bottle and at the same time the bottle also flew but in the opposite direction, falling to the wooden floor with a thud.

It was a subconscious reflex that made me shout "Fuck!" and the room went silent with all eyes upon me. I rescued the fallen bottle.

The manager came over to me and whispered in my ear "Take it back down to Robert".

I hurried back down to the cellar, telling Rob what had just happened.

"I shouted 'FUCK' and they all heard!"

He laughed heartily.

He unscrewed the cork from the corkscrew, telling me not to worry, I wasn't going to be sacked.

"The bottle was wet" I said. "That's why it slipped!"

He put the cork back in the bottle so that it could now be pulled out by hand. Fortunately, and with no knowledge of how I'd done it, I'd managed to rescue the bottle, spilling hardly a drop.

I took the bottle back up to the diners, pulled out the cork by hand, and told the happy couple how "terribly sorry" I was.

"Accidents happen" said the man, with a smile.

They said nothing about it being the very same bottle that I had dropped only minutes ago.

They said nothing about me opening the bottle by hand.

They said nothing about my swearing.

At the end of their meal they left me a huge tip.

I didn't get fired.

All in all it had been a fantastic day.

With the large tip in my pocket I finished my evening's work.

Rob and I put on our jackets.

"Do you fancy a drink?" asked Rob.

"It's too late now, isn't it?" I asked.

"I can take you to a place" he said.

He took me to the Tower.

As we strolled on icy streets towards the Tower Rob chatted easily.

"Me and Al just bought a house" Rob told me. "We're having a house warming party. You and Roger are more than welcome to come".

I explained that I was so busy with my various jobs that it all depended on which night of the week his party fell.

Rob told me the party was on a Saturday, in a few weeks time.

"Try to be there" he said.

The Tower doesn't exist anymore, but in those days it was a venue which serviced the Gay, Lesbian, Bisexual and Transgender community.

It might surprise people to know that the community thrived back in those days, although it was still somewhat underground.

We got past the doormen and headed upstairs to the Tower.

I bought the first round of drinks out of my tips. One for Al too, if we found him.

Al was on the dance floor, (dancing in the way that only a burly merchant seaman might dance).

Rob signalled to Al that we'd got him a drink.

Al danced across the floor to us and kissed Rob in a way that made me jealous; it was so easy, so casual, yet so passionate.

Theirs was an open relationship, which meant that they were both free to do what they wanted with whoever they wanted.

These extra curricula activities were few and never threatened the love they had for each other.

At least this is the way it seemed to me.

Their love for each other was obvious.

I was jealous.

I asked them what the secret was, one time.

Honesty, they told me.

Well, who would have known it was as simple as that?

I looked at Rob and Al and saw that both were completely comfortable with who they were.

They made no excuses.

They were complete human beings, and I longed to be like them.

I believed that if I ever found another human being who could love me for ME then I might finally be complete.

"So how's your love life?" Al asked me with a wink.

I thought of Farnham.

"I think I'm falling in love" I told him.

"Good for you. Anyone I know?" he asked, looking around hoping to catch a glimpse.

"You'd never see him in here Al. He's divorced, with a kid, probably straight."

"Do you know the difference between gay and straight?" he asked.

"Enlighten me".

"Three beers" he told me, laughing.

The club would be closed in minutes.

All three of us were very drunk by now.

I suggested a night cap back at our apartment.

The apartment was empty except for Roger.

"Hi honey" he said effeminately, even though he was always the most masculine of men.

He sometimes liked to pretend that he and I might be a couple, although ours was only ever the purest of friendships.

Roger had only just got home from a night in Reds.

Rob told Roger about the mishap at Harold's House earlier.

Some people can tell a story so well it's like you were there, and with such humour too.

Rob had this gift.

Al and Roger took several minutes to recover from their laughter.

I laughed too; a proper belly laugh.

"You shouted "Fuck" at your customers? You didn't get the sack? How do you get away with shit like that?" Roger wanted to know.

"I got a great tip too" I told him.

Al was telling Roger "your boyfriend, Charlie here, tells us he's in love".

"Who is it this time?"

"He won't tell us" Al explained. Three pairs of eyes questioned me, but I couldn't just spit it out like that.

"You'll think I'm mad Roger" I said.

"So! Spill!"

There was a dramatic pause, then I said the name "Farnham".

This must have explained a lot to Roger because he just went "Ah, I see now".

"What do you see?"

"Nothing!" he said. "Anyway, you know he's married and straight?"

"Divorced" I corrected.

"Separated!" he said. "I would have thought you had better taste than that. He's a bit old for you, isn't he?"

"He's thirty eight" I said.

"Way too old" he added. "You don't stand a chance, you DO know that, don't you?"

"Shut up" I laughed.

I got enough beer from the fridge to give our guests, and one each for me and Roger.

I told them the story about the salt in the coffee machine. They laughed.

Rob especially laughed his big hearty laugh and called me an idiot.

"Why?" I asked him.

"Your boss had you put salt in the coffee to get people to drink more booze. Salt makes you thirsty! Thirsty people drink more booze! You must have overdone it with the salt!"

"Oh" I said, finally getting it.

"Are you and Roger coming to our house warming?" he asked.

"Sure" we said.

"I have an early start tomorrow guys, so this will be my last beer, but you're welcome to stay" I told them.

I drank my beer, and then I was off to my double bed, hugging each friend goodnight. I was asleep within minutes. It had been such a long and eventful day.

"Charlie, wake up". It was Roger, gently shaking me back into consciousness.

"What's up?"

"I've been an idiot" he said. "Rob went home but Al stayed. I took him into my bedroom thinking I'd try out being gay!"

"Oh. What happened?"

"It's not for me. I'd be a really bad gay. The thing is that Al's still here though, and I don't know what to do."

"What do you want me to do?"

"I told him I thought my drink had been spiked with some acid or something, so he thinks I'm freaking out because of that. Problem is that he wants to 'daddy' me or something and I can't get rid of him. Can you get him out without hurting his feelings?"

"Leave it to me" I said, throwing on jeans and heading towards Roger's room.

Al was stretched out on Roger's double bed.

"Is Roger all right?" Al asked.

He sounded understandably concerned.

"He'll be fine Al, I just think he needs to sleep."

Al was naked, and not in the least ashamed of his body. Why should he be ashamed?

His burly frame was well muscled as if he might once have modelled for a Michaelangelo statue.

I tried to look Al only In the eyes but this was impossible. Every inch of his body was faultless.

His broad chest was hairy but not Neanderthal, and his erect nipples were perfect and pink. His thighs and calf muscles were larger than any I'd ever seen before.

It was a struggle not to look.

"Are you asking me to leave?" he asked.

I didn't answer him immediately.

"I think so Al, I'm sorry".

"No problem" he said.

Al picked up his clothes and carried them into the front room, ready to change into them.

I followed him into the front room.

Al threw his clothes onto the couch and turned to me.

He came towards me, and I didn't back away.

He pulled me into his huge arms and kissed me deeper than I'd ever been kissed before.

I found myself exploring his back, then his chest, kissing him all the time.

Al pulled away and said "You have an early start tomorrow", and he started to put all his clothes on.

He pulled on his boots, then his jacket, then kissed me again before going out the front door.

Roger was lying in my bed.

"Has he gone yet?" Roger asked.

"Yep, he's gone, you're in the clear."

"Was he all right about everything?"

"He seemed fine about it".

"Thanks buddy, I owe you one" he said and headed for his own room.

I went back to bed, but this time I couldn't get to sleep immediately.

I was confused.

Was I in love with Farnham or not?

If I was in love with Farnham then I wouldn't have felt that way as Al held me in his big arms and kissed me.

Surely I wasn't in love with Al!

There was no doubt that Al was a beautiful man, but Al was with Rob.

They were the ideal couple.

Finally, in spite of all my confusion, I must have dropped off to sleep.

Chapter Two

It was Tuesday the fifteenth of January.

I was working at Harold's House.

I was chatting to Rob while he fetched me a bottle of wine for some diners.

"How's Roger?" he asked.

"Fine" I answered.

"I mean, after his recent acid trip, or whatever it was?"

"Yeah, he freaked out a bit last night all right".

"Al was really worried about him" he said.

"I know Rob, but all Roger really needed was sleep," I told him.

"Funny. I never knew anyone who could sleep while on an acid trip".

"I'm not sure it was acid" I said.

"I'm not sure it was acid either" he said, and there was a deeper meaning behind his look, his words, which I couldn't fathom.

"Anyway, he's fine now".

Rob shook his head saying "You really are one of life's innocents, aren't you?"

I didn't know what he meant.

"THAT'S what I mean" he said, but I still didn't understand.

"You take everything at face value. Like the salt in the coffee."

"Mm" I muttered.

"Just make sure you don't get played, that's all".

"Who's going to play me Rob?"

"Just wise up. I don't want to see you hurt" and he squeezed my arm.

It was Thursday the seventeenth of January.

Time for Theory with Farnham.

"Good afternoon, boys and girls" he greeted us all.

"Now does anyone have their assignment prepared?"

A few hands went up, including my own.

Doctor Farnham picked on Elizabeth Summer who passed round copies of her chorale. Doctor Farnham played our starting notes, counted us in, and we began to sing. The chorale she had written was rather pretty but not astounding.

Doctor Farnham looked at the manuscript and said "Your counterpoint is flawless Mrs Summer, congratulations. I think it deserves a round of applause".

We clapped warmly, and Elizabeth smiled demurely with her head bowed.

Von Chanel was next.

He was a French Canadian from Quebec who was
majoring in violin, but he also a demon on the guitar. He,
like Elizabeth, was also a mature student, aged about
twenty seven. He was wire thin with wide eyes and a quick
sense of humour.

Von's chorale was simple and sweet. The sweetness, even I
could see, was because of too many consonances in the
melodies and harmonies.

(A consonance is a sweet sounding interval, and an
interval is the distance between two notes).

Nevertheless it was a good effort.

Doctor Farnham pointed out the abundance of consonances
but told Von he had grasped the basic rules nevertheless,
and Von beamed proudly.

Next up was Roger.

Roger, my flat mate and friend.

He was majoring in voice, although he was a phenomenal
pianist too.

We sang Roger's chorale and it was a perfect expression of
his personality; jolly and masculine. It was more like
Gilbert and Sullivan than Bach, but it followed all the
rules.

Doctor Farnham was pleased,

Roger got a warm round of applause.

Finally it was time to show the world MY chorale.

I passed round the thirty or so photocopies of my chorale.

Doctor Farnham played the four notes of the opening C
minor chord.

He then counted us in.

They sang, and it was breathtaking.

Alas, and did my saviour bleed?
And did my sovereign die?

Would he devote his sacred head
For sinner such as I?

There was a moment of hush when it ended, and then
sudden spontaneous applause, louder and warmer than
anything before.
I was crying just a little bit, with the joy of it, and wiped
my eye so that no one could see.
It had sounded so beautiful, and had been sung so well.
Roger patted me on the back then squeezed my shoulder.
Doctor Farnham let the applause die out of its own accord
and then spoke.
"Boys and girls, ladies and gentlemen, I have to explain
that a copy of this chorale was handed to me last week. In
my ignorance I humiliated the composer telling him to go
away and come back once he had corrected his parallel
fourths. This is a wonderful piece of work. Please accept
my sincerest, and most public, apology, Mr Watson".
Then Doctor Farnham made a slight bow in my direction,
and started to clap.
The rest of the class began clapping again.
The bell rang signifying the end of the lecture.
People began to leave for the next lecture.
I began to collect the photocopies of my chorale.
Doctor Farnham came over to me and said "I wonder if
you'd allow me to make it up to you by taking you out
somewhere".
"You don't need to make anything up to me" I said.
"I was very dismissive of your chorale. I should have
looked beyond the counterpoint. I should have recognised
its beauty. I would like to take you out somewhere".
I put the last of the photocopies away.
"I would love that" I said.

I know that I must have been grinning like an idiot, and that my eyes would have been sparkly with recent tears.

"How about tonight?" he asked.

I told him I was working.

I didn't go into detail about all my various jobs.

I just said that I'd be working.

"Tomorrow then?" he asked, and so our 'date' was arranged.

Anything I say to describe how I felt at that moment, and for the rest of the day, will be understatement. The strangest thing, though, is that when I remember that day the clearest and purest moment of joy was not in Doctor Farnham's praise. The joy was at its peak for the duration of my Chorale's first and only performance.

That night I had the strangest dream.

I dreamed that Duffy, and my mother's three other dogs, were all in the back of a yellow car which was parked on a mountainside.

The dogs were barking hysterically.

Outside the car, stripped to the waist, was an impossibly muscular axeman, sweat made his arms and chest glisten.

He had a black hood covering his face.

He was hacking at the car with his axe, and broke the rear window.

The dogs were barking louder now.

I felt helpless, only able to observe the axeman as he swung his broad shining axe at the car's rear window, his hugs muscles still glistening with sweat.

A phone rang incongruously..

It took several rings before I realized I was dreaming and the phone was beckoning me back to the waking world.

The phone was beside my bed.

I answered it.

It was my mother.

"Are you awake dear?" she asked.

"Only just. You woke me up from a dream."

"Sorry dear" she said. "Anyway, are you all right for me to pick you up tonight after your lectures?"

"Tonight?" I asked.

"Yes, tonight!" her voice was that of someone explaining the simplest thing to an idiot.

She was picking me up so I could begin my teaching of Mrs Van Nord's students.

I told my mother about my dream.

"I just want you to make sure that the dogs are safe when you come to pick me up" I explained.

"Oh they'll be safe dear. They can't get out of the dog-run out at the back here, the fencing is heavy duty!" she said proudly.

This put my mind at rest.

I prepared for my day of Kabalevsky practice and study and lectures.

I knew there was something I was forgetting.

Then, during the Theory lecture, it occurred to me that I was meant to go on a date with Doctor Farnham tonight.

At the end of his lecture I spoke to Doctor Farnham explaining that I'd just got a call from my mother and that I had to postpone our date.

"That's okay" he said. "Is Sunday any good to you?"

"I'd look forward to that, thanks for understanding."

He smiled at me then, looking directly into my eyes. I felt all the warmth return to me, and I was falling back in love with him. There was no question about it.

I'd finished the third hour of Kabalevsky practice and I was back home in the apartment now.
I was ready to be picked up and taken to my mother's home.
She lived about thirty miles outside of the city.
With snow and ice on the roads it would take about an hour to get there.
There was the toot of a car horn outside. I looked out of the first floor window and saw my mother's yellow Ford.
In a minute I was in the passenger seat.

"You remembered about the dogs, didn't you?" I asked.
I remembered my dream.
"They'll be absolutely fine in the dog-run" she reassured me.
She wanted to know about my week. I told her about the chorale and about the Kabalevsky.
We stopped at a gas station, though I could see that the tank still had plenty of fuel.
More snow was falling, and it was settling. My mother drove very carefully, and eventually we were less than a quarter mile from her house. Ahead was a large white shape, against a white background of snow, lit by the Ford's headlights. It was Annabel, the huge Mountain dog. My mother slowed the car.
"How did SHE get out?" my mother exclaimed.
I got out of the car, grabbed Annabel by the collar and told my mother to head on home.
If Annabel was out of the dog-run then the other dogs were loose too. It was better for her to get back home immediately to check on their safety, and I could walk Annabel back the quarter mile.

It took a while but I managed to get myself and Annabel back home.

Outside my mother's property, sitting on the dry stone wall, were three kids, young boys. They were no more than ten years old. They were all crying.

"Do you own a black dog?" the biggest one asked me.

"Yes. What's happened?"

Tears were running down his cheeks and his nose was snotty.

"The black dog was crossing the road to go into the woods" he said, pointing. "This big truck came round the corner and ran him over. Ran right over him. Then drove on. Your black dog was hurt real bad. He crawled into the woods." The kid was still pointing across the road into the darkness of the woods.

I quickly dragged Annabel into the house and slammed the front door behind her. The yellow Ford was parked in the driveway but there was no sign of my mother.

I ran into the woods.

It was dark.

It took a minute or two for my eyes to adjust.

Eventually I saw a dark shape at the foot of a tree.

It was Duffy.

I picked up his poor broken body in my arms and carried him back across the road. He was still conscious, but only just.

I whispered into his ear, telling him he was a good boy and that everything was going to be all right.

The next hour or so went by in a blur.

My mother drove us to a vet's place, which was nearby, thankfully.

The vet said he would pump Duffy full of something that would hopefully stop the internal bleeding.

He would keep Duffy in overnight, but we should really prepare ourselves for the worst.

It was unlikely Duffy would survive; there was too much internal damage.

Anyone who knows me will testify that I love all animals but especially dogs. Of all the dogs in the world I loved Duffy the most.

He died in the middle of the night, in a vet's surgery, all alone.

The next day I taught all Mrs Van Nord's students, though there was no joy in me.

I was in a black mood.

Bette, having heard about Duffy, came straight to Mrs Van Nord's house, and gave me the warmest of hugs.

"All dogs go to Heaven, you DO know that don't you?" she said.

By now I couldn't stop the tears from streaming down my cheeks.

"If you're still able to play the organ tomorrow I'll see if I can find a suitable sermon. I know I have something that will make you feel better".

The next morning I played the organ in the church, as I would do every Sunday.

Bette read her sermon, but I can't remember her words right now. I only know that they were touching and relevant.

I played the hymns, to a packed congregation, all without joy.

By now we had figured out that Annabel had pulled the dog-run's 'heavy duty' chain link fence right off the ground in her bid to escape.

Annabel was a strong dog as well as wilful!

All the dogs had followed her out of the hole she'd made. The littler dogs, Nemo and Henry, hadn't ventured off the property, but Duffy had wanted to explore the woods across the road. It had been his last exploration.

On Sunday evening, after church, my mother drove me back to the city.

"You knew that was going to happen, didn't you?" she said.

"What are you talking about?"

"You told me to look after the dogs. You knew Duffy was going to die".

I realized at that moment that the dream I'd had was a premonition.

What is the use of a premonition? If it comes true then, by definition, you couldn't have changed anything. If it doesn't come true then it's not a premonition.

"You have a gift, dear" my mother said.

"It doesn't feel like a gift" I said.

I was back at my apartment. I called Doctor Farnham.

"Listen, I might not be the best of company tonight" I explained.

"What's happened?"

"My dog, Duffy, died."

"I'm so sorry Charlie."

"Thanks. But maybe we should give it a miss tonight; I'd just depress you. We may have to leave it for another night."

"It sounds to me like you could do with cheering up. And besides, it might do you some good to talk about it. I know what it's like to lose a dog you love. Not everyone gets that, but I do."

I made more excuses, but Doctor Farnham became more insistent.
Eventually I surrendered to him.
"I'll pick you up in half an hour" he said.
Sometimes it really feels like you have no choice in the matter.

Doctor Farnham was punctual, as I imagined he would be. I was still desperately upset at the loss of Duffy, and I honestly believed that I would be lousy company, but the thought of an evening with Doctor Farnham made the pain seem less.

There was a very exclusive restaurant called the Montmartre, up on the hill. Doctor Farnham took me there. I had money in my pocket, from my lessons, but I was reluctant to blow it all on a meal and a bottle of wine. I had suggested Harold's House, or the Fisherman's Rest, because I knew I could get a staff discount at either place. Doctor Farnham wanted to take me somewhere more memorable; not to a place where I waited tables.
When you wait tables you're aware of how other waiters do their jobs. At Montmartre our waiter was more elegantly dressed and mannered than most of my diners. His accent, as you'd imagine, was French. Doctor Farnham surprised me by conversing with our waiter, Daniel, in perfect French. He ordered Tornados Rossini for us both, accompanied by a bottle of Jameson's Run, a fine Australian red.
When Daniel opened the bottle without dropping it and shouting "Fuck" I was mightily impressed.

"Duffy sounds like he was a beautiful animal" began Doctor Farnham.

"He was the best. More human than most humans I know". I explained how Duffy was rescued as a puppy. He'd been in our family for about twelve years.

"Then he's been with you for over half your life! No wonder this has had such an effect on you".

It was good to talk about my loss, and good to know that Doctor Farnham understood so completely.

I kept on calling my fellow diner 'Doctor Farnham' and eventually he said "You know you can call me Des, I really prefer it."

So I called him Des and he called me Charlie.

"I'm at a turning point in my life Charlie. I recently separated from my wife, whom I believed I loved but I think now I was mistaken. We have a beautiful boy, Nicholas, who I don't deserve in my life. I'm fast approaching middle age, and in spite of everything I feel I have nothing of any value, and that I am not valued. I see you, and the love you have for a dumb animal, and I wish I could feel as deeply as you do. I hear your chorale and I see all the passion that I wish I had. You lack a certain skill and finesse, but that will come in time. And in spite of all those things you lack you still have a grasp that I can only dream of."

"Flattery, Des, will get you me, if you're not careful"

"I believe your flirting with me Charlie. Are you?"

"I thought you were flirting with me!" I said truthfully. The wine was having the most wonderful effect. Even my grief was adding to the delicious moment.

"But yes," I said, "I think I AM flirting with you. Is that okay? Do you mind?"

Des grinned broadly, like a schoolboy.

"As I said, Charlie, I'm at a turning point. And no, I don't mind that you're flirting with me. I find it very flattering that a handsome young man like you would flirt with a middle aged man like me."

Des ordered another bottle from Daniel, again in perfect French.

"Your French is impeccable" I told him.

"It's really only good enough to order wine" he laughed.

"I'm sure it's better than that. I can order beer in virtually any language!"

"Charlie, beer is beer in any language. Apart from Spanish, where it's cerveza."

"So what about your turning point? What does that involve exactly?"

"I'm not sure EXACTLY, but I feel, know, that it must mean experiencing new experiences. That might mean travel, or music, or even love".

His eyes, I noticed, were the most magnetic blue. He wore glasses, as one would expect of a scholar, but beneath his glasses his eyes were beautiful.

I raised my glass to him and said "To travel then, and music."

"And even love?" he said, raising a glass to me in return.

"Now you are definitely flirting with me Des." I said.

"And do you mind?"

"I WILL mind if all it ever amounts to is flirting" I said, amazed at my boldness.

"I get the feeling that you might be more experienced in these matters than I am Charlie. I've only ever been with one person in my entire life; my wife".

"Are you serious?"

"Never more so. You think that's strange, or old fashioned?"

"No, just surprising. You seem worldly wise."

He chuckled at that.

"Perhaps I'll learn that kind of wisdom, with this turning point. But I might need a teacher".

"And you think I might be that teacher?"

"I'd like you to be" he said simply.

"Would you mind if we skip dessert?" I asked him.

"Are you okay? Are you feeling sick? God, I should have thought, what with you losing Duffy and everything."

"No, it's not that. I want you to take me home, to your place."

He smiled.

"I don't want to appear to be so, um," I struggled for the word, "slutty, but the thing is that I've had the biggest crush on you, for the longest time. And tonight I'd just like to be alone in your company. Nothing more, unless you want to."

"I'll take you home Charlie."

Des called Daniel over to our table.

Des paid for the meal with a credit card.

Daniel returned to our table a little while later.

"Je suis desolee Monsieur, votre Carte est refusee" he whispered in an undertone.

I had money on me, from my piano lessons.

I paid for our meal.

Des promised me solemnly that he would pay me back. It was all some embarrassing mistake, he said.

It never occurred to me that things might be moving too fast, not even for a second.

Soon we were at his home. It was a one bedroom apartment in an exclusive looking building. We took the lift to the fourth floor.

There was a black grand piano in the centre of the room, and books of music piled on top.

"How did you get the piano in here?" I asked.

"It wasn't easy" he laughed. "I had to hire a crane. It was expensive too!"

There was manuscript paper with music that Des was writing.

"My opera" he said. "One day I hope to finish it, and then you can hear it".

"I'd like that" I said. "What's it about?"

"You might find this interesting" he said. "Recently some divers discovered a German submarine wreck out in the harbour. They found theatre tickets on several of the bodies. Don't ask me how theatre tickets can stay intact underwater for all these years, but intact they were! The theatre was right here in town. These German submariners had visited our theatre, watched a show, and then set sail, only to be sunk by one of our ships."

Des went to the piano and softly played the piece he was working on.

The music conjured up an image of deep and cold waters, with the ghosts of men dancing with each other.

"It's wonderful" I said when he'd finished.

"There's a lot more work to do. In fact I'll need some help scoring for the individual instruments, if you'd like to get involved?"

"I'd like that" I answered, though I didn't really know what that might entail, or if I could find time.

"We can talk about all that later. In the meantime, I think you must be tired".

"Yes, I said. "I should get home".

"Not at all" he said. "I'd like you to stay".

"I couldn't stay Des!" I said, not shocked exactly, but surprised that Des was taking the lead like this.

"Why not?" he asked.

I couldn't think of a reason why not.

I thought about the situation for a moment.

"I could use a shower, if that's okay?" I said.

He showed me the bathroom, and I showered.

When I stepped out of the shower I saw that he'd laid out a bath robe made of thick towelling.

It was striped in thick bands of red, green and purple.

I slipped into the bath robe and emerged back into the living room.

Des was also wearing a matching bath robe.

He beckoned me to sit on his biggest chair.

My hair was still damp.

He came over to me and began to dry my hair with his fingers.

He just fingered my hair, gently, for fifteen minutes or so, until it was dry.

Then he started to massage the flesh at my shoulders and neck until I was completely relaxed.

"Is that nice?" he asked.

"Hmm" I moaned.

"It's time for bed, soldier" he said, and he guided me into his bedroom and onto his double bed.

He undid my bath robe slowly and then covered my naked body with his quilt.

He turned out the light and joined me in his bed.

His body was warm against mine as he put his arms around me.

At that moment I felt safer than at any other time.

I was happy just to fall asleep in his arms.
This was all the lovemaking we needed right now.
Anything more would have ruined the moment.

The next morning was a Monday and Des woke me with a
cup of freshly made coffee and a croissant.
"What's your plan today?" he asked.
"The usual. An hour of practice and then lectures" I
answered.
"You can practice here Charlie" he said.
I didn't have any of my music books.
"What pieces are you studying?" he asked.
I told him about the Kabalevsky.
"You're in luck" he said.
He left the bedroom, rummaged among his music books
and returned with a well worn copy of the Kabalevsky,
which had pencilled notes written in the margins and
across the staves.
"I studied this at University. I hope it helps".
"It really does! I can't tell you how much."
In the notes I noticed that, at the end of one crescendo,
there was the word EXPLODE in capitals.
All the other notes were equally as succinct and as useful.
I put on the multicoloured bath robe and carried the
croissant, coffee and Kabalevsky sheet music into the
living room, to the grand piano.
I opened up the music and began to play.
Des showered and dressed.
"Your first lesson is with me, at ten. Stay here till then.
Make yourself at home. I'll see you in an hour or so."
He kissed me on the forehead and went to leave.
I couldn't let him leave me with just a kiss on the forehead.
I got up from the piano and said "Des, before you go".

I hugged him close to me, and kissed him full on the lips, and finally let him go.

"Thank you" I said.

He smiled and said "I'll see you at ten sharp. Don't be late!"

It was Saturday.

It was the night of Al and Rob's house warming party.

Des had promised he could drive me to the church the next morning, in time for organ playing at Bette's church.

"How are we going to play this tonight?" asked Des.

I wasn't sure what he was saying.

"I'd prefer it if you introduced me, not as your lover, but as a friend".

I didn't have a problem with that.

Des was at his turning point.

I wasn't going to push him faster than he wanted to go.

Although Al and Rob had all heard me profess my love for Des, (that night in the Tower), no one knew our relationship had progressed.

As far as anyone knew we were just friends.

In retrospect Roger must have known something because I was spending nights away from the apartment we shared.

If he was aware of anything then he didn't say.

Des parked the car close to Rob and Al's new house.

It was at the end of a terraced block of houses, with a side entrance that lead onto a massive back yard.

The yard, we now saw, was overgrown but covered in festive fairy lights and Chinese lanterns.

I carried a pack of beer and Des had wine.

Rob met us in the back yard where Al was busy cooking over a barbecue.

Al had on an apron and chef's hat.

"Let me take those" Rob said, relieving us of the drinks. There were about ten people in the back yard, hovering around the barbecue.

I saw Roger who came straight over to us.

"Doctor Farnham" he said, beaming broadly and extending a hand in greeting.

"Please Roger, call me Des. We're not in school now".

I could see some of my fellow flat mates. There was Barb, Mick, Mark and Ursie Passion Flower.

I could hear a guitar. Von Chanel was playing it brilliantly. Von, recognizing his Theory teacher, gave Des a nod.

"I'd say things might get a bit wild later on. I hope you're ready" Roger said to Des.

"Wild is my middle name" he said.

This amused Roger, who gave me a wink.

Rob came back to the party, holding a bottle of beer for me, and a glass of wine for Des.

"Is this right?" he asked.

"Perfecto" said Des, "Thank you".

Des was properly introduced.

"Des" Rob said. "Charlie talks about you all the time. All good, which is a bit of a worry".

"He tends to see only the good in people. I can assure you I'm much more colourful than I've been painted".

Des and Rob seemed to hit it off like they were long lost friends, and I was relieved. It could have gone so badly, but it was going so well.

I was free to mingle a bit.

I crept up behind Al, still busy at the barbecue.

I gave him a bear-hug from behind, lifting him partly off the paved floor.

"Whoa there fella" he said.

Then he turned and saw it was me.

I hadn't seen Al since the night of Roger's 'acid trip'.
His face was expressionless, concentrated more on his
culinary efforts I guessed.
"Do you want a sausage?" he asked.
He had a plate filled with sausages he'd already cooked,
and offered me one.
I took it, and popped it into my mouth whole.
Al broke into laughter.
"Glad you could make it. Who's the plus one?"
"That's Des".
"Your lover?" Al asked.
"We're just friends".
"For now" he said. "Wait till he's had three beers."
"He's on the wine".
"Same deal. I want to give you the tour when I'm done
cooking".
"Okay. Do you want a beer or something?"
"Sure" he said. "But watch out. It'll be my third."
I fetched him a beer from the fridge in the kitchen where
Rob and Des were in mid conversation.
It was a deep discussion about Hitler.
It was pretty intense for party talk.
Rob was explaining "At the end of World War One Hitler
suffered hysterical blindness after a mustard gas attack.
Did you know that?"
"No, I wouldn't know a lot about that period of his life",
said Des with apparent interest. "I know he was a Lance
Corporal, and a second rate artist!"
"Well, all that's true. Anyway, he was taken to a hospital,
where he was treated for his hysterical blindness, by this
physician called Edmund Forster. I'm reading about it now.
Fascinating stuff. Until his treatment Hitler was a nobody.
After the treatment he became the Fuhrer."

"Really? I'm not familiar with any of this" said Des.

I couldn't tell if Des was just being polite.

"The book I'm reading suggests that Forster used various techniques to treat the hysterical blindness, which also resulted in Hitler's total belief in his own destiny. Until then he had no charisma of any kind".

I don't remember ever seeing Rob being quite so serious.

"So you're saying that this Edmund Forster CREATED a monster, that the Hitler we know about wouldn't have existed otherwise, if not for Forster??"

"Well, I'm not saying it! I'm just repeating what I read."

I got a beer and took it back to Al.

Al had nearly finished cooking all the meat.

"I'm a bit worried" I said. "Rob and Des are talking about Hitler! It all seems to be getting a bit heavy!""

"Best to leave them to it" he said. "Come on, I'll show you the house".

Then he bellowed in his deep voice "Come and get it y'all, while it's hot!"

I followed Al into the kitchen.

"Showing Charlie the house" he explained to Rob and Des.

"No worries" said Rob.

Al briefly showed me the rooms on the ground floor then escorted me up the stairs.

We went into the first room, a bedroom, and he closed the door behind us and locked it.

"Okay fella, you've been wanting this", he said.

He took off his chef's hat. Then he pulled off his apron, and then his T-shirt. Then he put his chef's hat back on, which amused me.

"What about Rob?" I asked.

"Rob's fine" he answered.

"What about Des?"

"You said you were just friends!"
His jeans were round his ankles now and he was pulling
my clothes off too.
I didn't want to be aroused, but I was.
The man I loved was downstairs talking about Hitler and I
was having wild abandoned sex with the chef.
It didn't feel right but I lost myself in the moment.

It didn't last much longer than five minutes.
I don't need to, or want to, go into graphic detail here.
I'd like to use be able to use the excuse that a lot of
adulterers use; that it meant nothing.
That would be a lie though.
Those five minutes passed too quickly yet seemed to last
an eternity.
Every second of that time represented countless different
extreme emotions.
For every question there was an answer, and the answer
was always 'surrender to this moment, there may never be
another'.

We dressed quickly, once our furtive deed was done.
Al still had his hat on. It's an image that will stay with me.
With no other word between us we went back downstairs.
Rob and Des were still in the kitchen, still discussing
Hitler.
Rob was telling Des "and Forster was found dead in his
bathroom, apparently having shot himself with a gun that
no one knew he possessed".
Des was still showing immense interest.
"You lost your apron" Rob said to Al.
"I finished cooking".
"Your still wearing your hat!"

Al adjusted the hat and grinned.

Rob smiled at me, and I suddenly realized that this had probably all been planned in advance.

I saw now that Rob and Al might have guessed that Des was going to be my plus one, and that there was more to our 'friendship' than I'd let on.

I knew now, with a fair amount of certainty, that Rob's discussion with Des about Hitler had been choreographed, to keep Des from going upstairs to find me.

I remembered how Rob had warned me not to 'be played', and saw that he had actually been 'playing' me himself.

Could any of this be true?

I was almost certain that it COULD be true.

The question I asked myself was 'did I care?' and the answer was 'no, I was fine with it all'.

I looked at Des and realized that he had no clue as to what had happened upstairs, despite his huge intellect, despite his love for me.

Mick came into the kitchen then, exhaling the smoke from a huge joint made from his home-grown grass.

The grass that grew in my cupboard!

The cupboard in my room had been lined with silver foil and a brooder bulb fitted. The resulting environment was perfect for growing weed.

Mick passed the joint to me. I looked at Des.

Des had no idea I sometimes smoked weed.

His expression told me he didn't mind, so I took the joint and had a deep toke on it.

Maybe I'd misread Des's expression.

I'd misread a lot of things.

A joint was definitely NOT going to clarify things, but I was beyond caring at that moment.

"Von wants you to sing something for us" Mick said to me.

Von was aware I could hold a tune, and he was proficient enough on the guitar to back me, so I left Al, Rob and Des in the kitchen and headed for the sound of music in the back yard.

"Thanks Charlie," Von said. "I was running out of tunes. I need you to help me out."

"No problem" I said.

"What do you want to sing?"

For some reason I thought 'Tracks of My Tears' might be appropriate.

There were about thirty people in the yard now, or maybe more. It was in full swing. Everyone seemed to join in on the chorus and by the end of the song I'd won my audience over. I sang 'Under the Boardwalk' next,

Mick handed me another joint and before too long I was very high.

Des brought me another beer while I sang.
He seemed to be in good spirits.
All I wanted to do was forget, for the moment, what had happened upstairs less than half an hour before.
The drink, the grass, the singing, all helped me to forget.
Even if it was just for a short while.

My small audience, now thirty people, were appreciative. I was ready to leave the spotlight now, but there were shouts of 'More, more' so I felt obliged to sing just one more.

I had an idea.

A while ago I had written some music for a favourite poem by Keats, 'La Belle Dame Sans Merci'.

I told Von the chord sequence, and he ran through it a couple of times.

Then I began to sing.

Oh what can ail thee knight at arms
Alone and palely loitering?
The sedge is withered from the lake
And no birds sing

Oh what can ail thee knight at arms?
So haggard and so woebegone
The squirrel's granary is full
And the harvest's done

I see a lily on thy brow
With anguish moist and fever dew
And on they cheek a fading rose
Fast withereth too

I met a lady in the meads
Full beautiful a faery's child
Her hair was long and her foot was light
And her eyes were wild

I made a garland for her head
And bracelets too and fragrant zone
She looked at me as she did love
And made sweet moan

I set her on her pacing steed
And nothing else saw all day long
For sideways would she lean and sing
A faeries' song

She found me roots of relish sweet
And manna wild and honey dew

And sure in language strange she said
"I love thee true"

She took me to her elfin grot
And there she wept and sighed full sore
And there I shut her wild, wild eyes
With kisses four

And there she lulled me asleep
And there I dreamed, ah woe betide
The latest dream I ever dreamed
On the cold hillside

I saw pale kings and princes too
Pale warriors, death pale were they all
They cried "La belle dame sans merci
Hath thee in thrall"

I saw their stark lips in the gloam
With horrid warning gaped wide
And I awoke and found me here
On the cold hillside

And this is why I sojourn here
Alone and palely loitering
Though the sedge is withered from the lake
And no birds sing

Von followed me perfectly, slowing down slightly as we reached the end.
There was a moment of silence, then spontaneous cheers, applause, and shouts of appreciation.
Loudest in the small crowd was Des.

I was aware it was getting late now, and that I had a church organ to play the next day.
Des was happy to drive us both back to his home.
"I'll see you back at the apartment" Roger said.

"Maybe" I said. "I might be asleep already."
"If you are I won't wake you buddy".
I said goodbye to everyone.
Al insisted on giving me a big bear-hug.
I knew now that I was being played, didn't care, and hugged him back.

"I like your friends" Des said, once we were on the road. "Especially Rob. He's fascinating".
I didn't want to tell Des that every fascinating thing Rob had said might have been scripted, just to keep Des from going upstairs.
"I think it might be a good idea if we had some sort of party of our own" he said. "Perhaps a dinner party. Maybe invite Roger, Rob and Al. Maybe we can make an announcement?"
"What announcement?" I asked.
"I was thinking I'm ready to let just a few people know, (not the whole world, just a few people we can trust), that you and I are more than just friends".
This was something I had longed to hear, but right now it just seemed to complicate everything.
I know that I should have chosen that moment to tell Des everything about what had happened upstairs at the house warming party, but something stopped me.
"You're sure this is something you want to do? This announcement, I mean," I said.
"I love you Charlie. I don't know where that road is going to take us, but I know it's a road I want to travel down. All I know is that I'm only going to be happy travelling that road with you".
This made me want to cry, and some of those tears would have been from pure love, and some out of guilt.

What could I do?

"Des, I love you too."

"So it's settled. We'll have a party, invite some of your friends, let them know?"

"Sure" I said. "Let's do it".

The next morning Des drove me to Bette's church.

My mother, thankfully, wasn't there.

She wasn't likely to go to Bette's services without Riff, and he was at sea.

It would have been difficult to explain Des, and I wasn't ready for it right now, with my sore head.

I was feeling worse for wear after the party but that didn't greatly affect my hymn playing.

Des sat in the congregation, which was another major step for him.

He seemed happy to be introduced to Bette.

I introduced him as my friend and mentor, and that avoided too many difficult questions.

Bette's sermon, that day, was about Truth.

It was all especially poignant for me since I was caught in a web of deceit now.

At the end of the service Bette invited us both for Sunday lunch.

We declined, saying we'd been to a party last night.

"Hangover?" she asked.

"Afraid so" I told her.

"You're only young once I suppose" she said, without judgement. "By the way, did you notice the new carpet in the church?"

I had noticed it.

She'd replace the threadbare blue with a vibrant red.

"Isn't red supposed to be a sinful colour or something?" I asked her.

"Don't be silly" she said. "How can a colour be sinful?"

"Well it's very bright anyway" I told her.

She laughed.

"That must have been some party" she said.

She kissed us both goodbye, telling Des how pleased she was to have met him.

Driving back to the city Des said "You've been so busy, with work, school and everything, and I haven't had time to share everything with you".

His tone was light but I felt the dread that all guilty people must feel.

"Go on" I encouraged.

"Well, I was thinking. I have family in Ireland. Do you have a passport? Of course you do".

"Yes, I have a passport. It's only a year old".

"Good. I thought it might be a nice idea to take a break. Go visit the Emerald Isle. What do you say?"

"I'd say it sounds great, but does that mean you're going to introduce me to your family as your lover?" I asked him.

"I hadn't thought that far ahead. I just thought that you're under a lot of stress with everything going on, and it would be good to get away".

It was true.

I'd begun to have memory lapses.

I was feeling the pressure.

I'd noticed that there were times I got my restaurants mixed up.

I'd be in Harold's House but think I was in the Fisherman's Rest, and vice versa. Other times I'd be doing my regular lunch-time practice but I'd be convinced I was doing my third practice of the day.

My morning practice wasn't usually an issue.

I was spending most mornings practicing on Des's grand piano.

Sometimes it was a struggle to remember what day of the week it was.

I'd kept a time-table so disaster was always avoided, but I had a feeling that one day I'd forget I even HAD a time-table.

I suppose it didn't help that Mick was now in the habit of giving me a small packet of grass every week.

He didn't want any money for it, (it was payment for letting him use my cupboard), and so I took it. And, of course smoked it.

I justified it by telling myself that I needed it to help me relax.

I was drinking every day these days too.

I guessed it was all taking its toll.

The Kabalevsky was proving to send me on a nervous breakdown too, in spite of the pencilled notes Des had provided me, on his sheet music.

I had a recital coming up soon, and I was nowhere near ready for it.

Yes, a trip to Ireland might be the very thing.

"It sounds like a great idea" I told him.

"Also" he added "I was thinking that we could buy a house".

I was stunned to silence, just for a second.

"Okay" I said, with a question in my tone.

"It's just that, seeing Rob and Al so happy in their new place, it got me thinking".

"Is this all moving a bit fast?" I asked him.

"No, I don't think so. I mean, if you think about it, you're paying rent on a place and you hardly live there. I earn enough for the two of us anyway, (even including the allowance I give Sandra and the boy), and you could work less jobs. You wouldn't be running round all the time wondering what you were doing."

"Is it that obvious?" I asked.

"Well frankly, yes, it is. To me anyway. And I've noticed that your course work is suffering too. You're very bright and so it's easy for you to coast, and no one would ever know that you're not putting in a hundred per cent, but I notice. I expect more from you".

He saw I wasn't taking this too well.

"Charlie, the last thing I want to do is lecture you, because I love you and care about you, but maybe you need to hear this".

I was beginning to get angry now, but gritted my teeth.

"Like now, for example. You're angry, I can tell. And I'm not trying to make you angry. I'm only trying to help us make a proper life together. If we bought a house together you could, WE could, start to create our own happiness."

I knew what he was saying.

I knew he was making sense.

Even so, to me it just sounded like he was 'playing' me, and I was resistant.

I was NOT going to be played.

I was NOT going to be lectured.

"I knew I'd push you too far. Forget I said anything" he said.

"Can I start again?" he asked me.

He didn't wait for my answer.

"I just want you to see the logic in all this. The next step is for us to move in together, don't you think so?"

"You might be right" I answered.

"You know I'm right, there's no 'might' about it. Then you wouldn't have to work so hard, you could get on top of all the REAL things you need to do."

"What REAL things?" I asked.

"You wrote some beautiful music for that Keats poem, last night. When did you do that? I bet it wasn't recently."

"I wrote it a few years ago when I was..." I couldn't finish the sentence.

"When you were.. what?"

"It doesn't matter". I knew I sounded sullen, and there was nothing in the world I could do about it.

"Please talk to me" he begged.

"I wrote that when I was recovering from an 'episode', years ago" I told him.

"An episode? What's that?"

"A nervous breakdown, if you must know".

"Jesus Charlie, you never told me about that!"

"Would it have made a difference? Would you love me less?" I could feel tears welling up, but was determined to bury them.

"I could never love you less. You must know that? Tell me what happened".

So this is how I found myself telling Des about a very dark part of my history, a part that few people knew.

My mother had divorced her first husband, my father, Jim Watson.

I suppose I was about five years old when Jim began abusing me, sexually.

It's not something I care to remember, let alone talk about.

Yet here I was, telling Des.

I described Jim Watson, telling Des that we was a big, bald brute of a man, with tattoos, and the body of a power-lifter. He was the kind of a man who was used to getting his own way.

"The abuse carried on for another ten years. I couldn't tell anyone. I began to 'cut' myself. Do you know what I mean by that?"

"I can only imagine" Des said. "It must have been terrible."

"Terrible is just a word. Words mean nothing. I was in a very black place, suicidal. There was no escape from the abuse, the sex. I was less than a slave."

"Did your mother know?"

"Well" I was smiling slightly now. "That's the thing. She says she didn't know. Then she says she had a faint glimmer of an idea. Then she says she DID know and that she tried to stop it. Whatever she says it's just meaningless words, and HER words especially mean nothing. She will say whatever it takes to stay at the centre of attention. It doesn't have to be true."

"So what happened? How did it end?"

"It didn't really end, not in the sense that you mean. I couldn't tell anyone because I guess I was afraid no one would believe me. I knew that what was going on was wrong, but somehow I shouldered all the blame, believing that I was solely responsible for what was going on. It's very hard to explain."

"Go on" he urged.

"I threw myself into music, losing myself there. It was a kind of escape I suppose. Music became more real to me than the 'real world'. In the end I was unable to talk, unable even to move. I was sent to a series of doctors, specialists, who figured out that there was nothing physically wrong with me. To be honest I can't really remember too much about some of it. The doctors said it had to be psychological. It put a lot of stress on my parent's marriage and they divorced. I guess it's ironic that when Jim Watson was out of my life I gradually got better. Part of the healing process involved me writing. I wrote the music you heard, Keats, when I was recovering in hospital."

"What happened to this Jim Watson guy. He was an animal".

"No, he wasn't an animal. I have a lot of time for animals. Anyway, I'm sure there were reasons he was driven to abuse me. Maybe HE was once abused. You know that the Abused are very likely to become Abusers? Did you know that? It's true."

"No, I don't know very much about this kind of thing. I just wish there was something I could have done to prevent all that. I feel so helpless".

"Des, you're a very sweet man, and I wouldn't WANT you to know anything about this kind of thing. Anyway, you can't change what's already happened."

"You didn't answer me. What happened to this Jim Watson guy?"

I could tell Des was angry, not at me, but at this man from my past.

"No one really knows what happened to him as far as I'm aware. He moved to another town, and we lost track."

"Didn't you tell the police?"

"No. I only told my mother recently. At first she didn't believe me. It's not something you would WANT to believe I guess. But no, the police were never told. What would be the point?"

"Charlie, the point is that he's free to do the same thing to another child. How would you feel about that?"

I was silent.

I had often thought that Jim Watson might be abusing another child, or children, but I felt ineffectual. I felt I'd be disbelieved.

"We need to think about what we have to do" he said.

"Don't you understand Des? In this thing there is no WE. There was only ever ME and it's all in the past now."

"Charlie, 'WE' is ALL there is from now on. You're never going to be alone again. We face this together".

We were back in town now.

Des parked the car and we headed for the lift to his apartment.

We were silent all the way up in the lift.

The lift door pinged open and we were in the front room with the piano.

I made for the piano, instinctively, and began to play.

I played for a full hour, the Kabalevsky.

The frenzied first movement that symbolized the edge of madness.

Des let me play everything out of my system, occasionally bringing me fresh coffee.

"Can we talk?" he asked with great concern in his voice.

"Sure" I said.

From my tone I'd imagine no one would be able to guess any of the extreme emotions I was feeling.

Not least of these feelings was an inexplicable resentment that Des was choosing to meddle in my past.

I didn't count on Des's great perception.

"Sure?" he said, exactly copying my nonchalant tone. "What's THAT about?"

I shrugged.

"Do NOT push me away Charlie, because I am NOT going anywhere. You're stuck with me. Don't you get it yet?"

I said nothing.

Maybe I WAS trying to push him away, not realizing it consciously.

"Let's just forget for the moment about what you just told me. Let's forget about buying a house together. Let's forget about our trip to Ireland. Okay?"

"Okay" I agreed.

"Do you love me?"

"Of course I do" I told him.

"Then say it! Tell me you love me".

He sounded fierce and stubborn.

"God Des, this is ridiculous. I LOVE YOU" my voice was almost a shout.

"Come here" he said, his arms open, waiting to hold me.

I got up from the piano and went to him.

He held me tight, whispered, "it's all going to be okay. Do you believe me?"

This seemed to be the perfect trigger that unleashed a flood of emotion, and I began to bawl uncontrollably.

He kept whispering "do you believe me? It's all going to be okay."

I got my emotions under control.

"It's not all going to be okay Des. I love you, with all my heart. But it's NOT all going to be okay."

I tried to pull away but he held me close.

"I make you this solemn promise Charlie. I will fix this. You will be happy. WE will be happy. I want you to believe me. Can you believe me?"

"I can try" I said.

"No, that's not good enough. I need you to say it. I need you to say you believe me."

"I really want to believe you Des".

"Damn you Charlie, just SAY it!"

I took a deep breath.

"I believe you".

By now I wasn't quite sure what things I'd agreed with Des.

I knew we were having a dinner party, that much I DID recall.

Plans for the dinner party were advanced enough that Roger, Al and Rob had accepted the invitation.

It was also decided that I would be in charge of the kitchen.

Of the two of us it transpired that I was a slightly better cook.

The party was arranged for a Friday night.

At four o'clock on the Friday afternoon in question I was beginning my Kabalevsky practice.

I had long known that Miss Clokovsky's expectation that the piece would be ready after just one week was a bit optimistic.

She was not well pleased about that.

While I practiced there was a pot roast in the slow cooker, chocolate desserts in the fridge and plenty of wine and beer.

Everything was under control, but then I guess that's how I do things.

There was the sound of a key in the front door.

It was Des, of course.

He wasn't alone.

With him was a black Labrador puppy, which rushed into the living room, tail wagging frantically, straight towards me.

It's funny really how a puppy, wagging its tail, can fill me with instant joy.

"What's this?" I asked.

"A puppy" replied Des.

"Well, I can see that" I said, bending down to the puppy and getting big licks for my trouble.

"He's yours. Ours" Des informed me. "What do you think".

"I love him. What's his name?"

"Richard".

"Richard? You have to be kidding me!"

"Yes, I'm kidding you. He hasn't got a name yet. You have to name him."

I don't know why but I immediately thought we might call him 'Scout'.

I told Des.

"Scout it is then" he said.

I thought about this for a minute.

What was Des thinking?

We couldn't look after a puppy!

"This is a mistake" I said. "We can't keep him".

Des said "I've been thinking about this. If you don't think we can keep him with us you can let your parents look after him. Maybe they'd like to fill the gap left by Duffy".

"Maybe" I said, still unsure.

Scout was still wagging his tail and still licking my face.

I was still filled with the joy that only a puppy can bring.

I knew it was too late.

We had to keep him.

Underlying everything was this feeling that Des was forcing me into a corner.

The trip to Ireland, the prospect of a new house, his thoughts on Jim Watson, and now the puppy.

I can't say that I was consciously thinking about this.

All I know is that the feeling was there, as yet still in my subconscious.

"If it makes a difference" said Des "I found us a dog-sitter. I know we're both busy but I figure a dog-sitter will make it easier".

"I just find it hard to believe you get a puppy and you don't tell me about it!" I said.

"I wanted it to be a surprise" he said.

It seemed he was totally unaware of how claustrophobic he was making me feel.

I was only just becoming aware of how claustrophobic he was making me feel.

"It's certainly a surprise" said I.

"Look" he said "Let's get tonight over with and we can decide what to do with Scout tomorrow".

I agreed, but in my heart I already knew Scout had found a home with us.

I wasn't completely happy about having the decision made for me, but none of that was Scout's fault.

"Until we decide what to do I'll go to the store and buy some dog food."

Des left me alone with Scout.

It seemed that the minute that Des left for the shop Scout started to growl at me, for no reason that I could fathom.

Scout backed away from me with his heckles raised.

He growled and then he barked.

I was down on my hands and knees now, extending one arm to him to try to calm him down.

Nothing that I did worked.

"What's the matter little boy?" I said to him gently.

I reached out to him again.

He snapped at my hand, drawing blood.

"Little bastard" I said, more to myself.

The growling, barking and now snarling continued until there was the sound of a key in the door.

Des let himself in.

"What's going on here?" Des asked.

The puppy ran to Des, making whimpering noises.

Des picked Scout up into his arms and put down the bag of dog food.

"I don't know what happened" I said.

I tried to explain to Des what happened, but it sounded unbelievable now that Scout was whimpering in Des's arms.

Des said nothing.

I knew what he was thinking.

He had accusing thoughts that he didn't want to say out loud.

He thought I'd done something to the poor little puppy.

"Honestly Des, I don't know what happened. I didn't do anything to make him like that. You DO believe me don't you?"

Des still remained silent.

I saw that he was feeling along Scout's hind leg.

The puppy yelped suddenly, in great pain.

"He's hurt himself somehow" Des said.

"I don't know how that happened" I said.

"Neither do I!" said Des. "He was fine when I brought him home. He was fine until I left him here with you!"

I couldn't believe what Des was implying.

"Des, I swear to you I would never hurt an animal, ever. You should know me well enough by now".

"Well, he's not fine now. I think he needs the vet".

Des left, without another word, carrying Scout.

I was suddenly very angry and hurt.

More than anything else I was in despair that I might have accidentally hurt Scout. Had I hurt the puppy somehow, without realizing it?

I paced round the apartment.

I couldn't face the piano.

I couldn't face working in the kitchen although all the catering had been done anyway.

I couldn't face anything.

I was suddenly at a dead end.

Then it occurred to me.

Wasn't there something that I could do?

Wasn't there such a simple thing that I could do that might get me back out of this dead end?

A very simple thing I remembered from years ago?

I went into the kitchen.

I went to the knife box and pulled out the sharpest knife.

I pulled up the sleeve on my left arm.

I found the meatiest part of my forearm and sliced into it.

There was an instant relief, and the blood began to flow.

The pain was like crystal and seemed to clarify everything.

I wrapped a sheet of kitchen towel around my arm, but there was too much blood for just one sheet.

I wrapped more kitchen towel around my arm.

It still wasn't enough.

I knew there had to be a bandage in the bathroom in the first aid kit.

I found it and wrapped it around my arm.

The blood stopped flowing eventually.

I found the little parcel of grass that Mick had recently given to me, and I rolled myself a joint.

Then I smoked it.

There was the familiar sound of a key opening the front door and Des let himself in. Scout wasn't with him.

"Where's Scout" I asked.

"The vet's going to keep him in. He has a fracture, but it can be fixed."

"Thank God" I said.

"The vet said it might have been an old fracture".

"MIGHT have been an old fracture? And what if it was a NEW fracture?" I asked.

"Listen Charlie, I'm not accusing you of anything. Let's just say that all that running around and tail wagging made an old fracture worse, and because he was in pain he took it out on you".

"Yes" I said. "Let's just say that!"

"For God's sake, don't be angry. I understand why you might be angry, but that won't achieve anything, will it?"

"No, you're right" I said, calming myself down a bit.

"Have you been smoking a joint?" he asked.

I should have guessed he'd be able to smell the weed.

I should have opened the balcony window.

"Yes I smoked a joint. I was fucking upset, all right?"

"Okay, sorry, let's leave it".

The bag of dog food was still on the floor where Des had left it.

He picked it up and put it in the kitchen.

"Is everything under control for tonight Chef?" He asked, changing the subject.

"Yes, I think so. All under control".

The thing is that things really weren't under control.

Not at all.

I heard Des ask me, from the kitchen "Is there blood on this knife Charlie?"

"Oh that's probably from the pot roast" I answered.

Des said nothing.

His silence made me think he didn't believe me.

I had the feeling that Des found it hard to believe anything I was saying now.

I could hear the sound of a tap running.

Dennis was rinsing the bloody knife.

"There's a lot of blood on some kitchen towels out here Charlie" he said. "Did you cut yourself?"

I didn't know how to answer, so I said nothing.

He came into the living room, clutching bloody kitchen towels.

"What's happening here Charlie?" he said and I could see great sadness in his beautiful blue eyes behind his glasses.

I realized Des might see my bandage, but I was beyond caring.

I found myself about to cry again, and this made me angry, with myself.

I buried my head in my hands and repeated over and over "I didn't hurt Scout. I would never hurt Scout".

Des came over to where I was sitting, and held me gently in his arms.

"It's okay Charlie. I believe you."

Chapter Three

I felt like the emotional equivalent of a wrung out old rag. Des suggested we cancel our dinner party but I thought we could struggle through the evening without anyone knowing about Scott's fracture, or any of the other secret things we were struggling with.

It was a little after eight o'clock and there was a buzz from the intercom.
Roger, Rob and Al were all together at the front door downstairs.
Des buzzed them in.
A minute or so later they were at the apartment door.

This was the first time any of them had seen the apartment.
It was quite impressive, especially with an elegantly dressed dining table and a grand piano.
Roger made straight for the grand piano and played something by Gershwin.
Rob and Al admired the view of the city from the balcony.

I got everyone a beer, and Des a glass of wine.
I had a joint already rolled and took it out to the balcony.
The smell of dinner filled the apartment deliciously.
The atmosphere appeared perfect for a night of civilized entertaining.
Des joined Roger at the piano and within minutes they were playing a Mozart symphony arranged for two hands.
They giggled like schoolboys.
I lit the joint and passed it to Al.
"So is this a special occasion?" he asked.
""All I can tell you is that Des has an announcement" I answered.
"Has he asked you to marry him?" Rob wanted to know.
This was ridiculous; at this point in history there was no such thing as gay marriage, except perhaps in Holland.
"I'm not telling. Des has to make the announcement. If I tell you then it's cheating!"
"Well it certainly sounds very intriguing. When does he make the announcement? I can't wait" said Al.

There was mischief in his voice and a twinkle in his eye.
"Well, you're just going to have to wait, but I guess it'll be soon" I said.
"I'll tell you something. I'm starving" added Al.
I guessed that Rob and Al could eat a lot, and then more.
So I'd made plenty.
As it was I didn't feel so hungry after all the emotion of the last few hours.
"Do we get a tour of the place?" Al asked me.
I remembered the last 'tour' I'd taken with Al.
He grinned when he realized what I was remembering.
"Sure you get a tour" I said, "but there's not a lot to see really".
Rob had finished the last of the joint, and threw it over the balcony.
"Show us anyway" he said.
I escorted them through the living room as if I was an estate agent.
"This is the main room where all the music is made" I said and then guided them into the kitchen.
There was no door between kitchen and living area.
It was almost open plan.
"Something sure smells good" said Rob.
Then I showed them into the only bedroom.
"This is more like it" said Al, closing the door behind us, dampening the sound of Mozart by a few decibels.
"Guys! What are you doing?" I asked, in a voice just a bit too high.
Rob had his bearded mouth on my mouth.
Al had me pinned up against the door and had a hand down the front of my jeans.
This was all too confusing, and too risky, and threatened to overturn everything.

I struggled against these two big men but it was useless.
Al was now chewing at my ear.
There was no denying that I was extremely aroused, no matter how much my mind was telling me NOT to be.
Al now had a hand down the BACK of my jeans, and his fingers were working their way towards my hole.
I clenched by butt cheeks hoping to block his path but he was just too insistent and too strong.
One of his fingers slid all the way in, and I must have grunted.
Al now had hands at the front and at the back of my jeans.
Rob was now chewing at my nipples.
He was gentle, and then rough, and then gentle again.
Suddenly the Mozart symphony had stopped.
Al and Rob didn't stop.
I could hear Des's voice now, asking if everything was all right.
I managed to take a breath and said "Okay guys, enough's enough" and they finally stopped.
"Well" said Rob. "That was fun" and Al chuckled.

"I thought we'd lost you" said Des when we all reappeared.
"Just taking the tour" said Al.
I decided that now would be a good time to serve the pot roast.
I made them all sit at the table, but Rob and Al were very difficult to control.
They were both full of mischief and I wondered if it was because of the joint.
The meal was served, and we all had a drink to go with it.
Des made a toast.
"To good friends".
We repeated the words.

"Eat! Everyone, enjoy" he said, like the consummate host.
Al and Rob tucked in straight-away with no further
encouragement needed.
Roger, on the other hand, said "so what's this
announcement?"
Al and Rob stopped eating for a second.
I was curious as to how Des planned to phrase his
announcement.

"If you give me just a second" Des said, and left the table,
and went into the kitchen.
He came back with a bottle of champagne that I didn't
know he possessed, and a tray of five champagne flutes.
"My God, it's serious" said Al.
Des popped the cork.
Then poured the champagne into the flutes.
We now each had a glass.
One thing I could say about Des is that he had class.
"I'd like us all to raise our glasses and toast New
Beginnings".
"New Beginnings" we repeated.
"As you may know I'm recently separated from my lovely
wife, Sandra".
Al raised his glass again and said "Sandra!"
"It was a turning point for me, as I told Charlie here. I was
about to embark on a new journey, with new experiences.
And I'd like to tell you, dear friends, that the person who
has agreed to join me on this journey is... Charlie".
"Hooray" said Al.
"Is this the surprise announcement?" asked Roger. "Didn't
you think we'd all guessed that by now?"
Des was puzzled.
"How did you guess?" he asked.

"Let me see now. Charlie missing from our apartment. No sign of him in the practice rooms early in the mornings. He hasn't been out your sight since you both got together. Everyone knew."

"Everyone?" Des seemed pained at this.

"No, not everyone. But everyone round this table. Oh, and Barb, Mark, Mick, and Ursie Passion Flower. I think Von guessed too but I can't be sure." Roger informed him.

"When did you all guess?" asked Des.

Al and Rob looked at each other.

Al said "It had to be the night of our house warming".

"Yes, that was it" said Rob.

"Oh shit" said Des. "So this was a big waste of time then?"

"No, don't think of it like that. We have food and drink, and good company. That's never a waste of time" said Rob.

"Anyway" said Al "I'm happy for you both."

"Hear hear" said Roger, raising his glass again.

"No one deserves it more than you two" added Rob.

"How would all those other people know? I don't even know them" asked Des.

"They were all at the party" said Al.

"And besides" said Roger, "I may have mentioned something. Don't worry. They're all the soul of discretion".

"Oh, I'm sure they are" said Des, looking very serious.

"Is this something you want to keep quiet? Is it just between us?" asked Roger.

"Well that was the idea" answered Des, "but I guess we can forget all about that now".

"I was just kidding you Des. I didn't say a word to the other guys, honest. But the three of us guessed. Anyway, your secret is safe, if you want it to be a secret" said

Roger. "And now that I have something on you I'm hoping you'll give me better grades".
Des smiled at this.
"I guess I have no choice" he said.
"Does this mean you and Des will be moving in together?" Roger asked me.
I didn't know how to answer this.
I looked at Des but he said nothing to help me out.
"We've talked about it" I answered.
"It makes sense for you to move in together" said Al.
"This place might be a bit too small for the two of you though" added Rob.
"Maybe you two could buy a house together, like Rob and Al here" said Roger.
"It's something we've discussed" said Des, and I could see he was trying to help me out.
"It's a great idea" said Al. "If you're serious about each other" he added.
"Okay! Okay guys! I get it" I interrupted. "You want us to have the fairytale happy ending. Fine, but it's not as easy as that".
"Why not? It's as easy as you want to make it" said Al.
"There are a few wrinkles that need to be ironed out before we decide what we're doing" said Des.
"Before we do anything we'll be taking a break, in Ireland" I said.
Des smiled at this news.
I was aware I hadn't mentioned our trip, and maybe Des thought I was against the idea, or that maybe I'd forgotten it completely.
This seemed to put us back on track.
Well, maybe not completely back on track, but some of the way.

"That sounds fantastic. I wish Rob would take me somewhere like Ireland" put in Al. "When are you going?" We hadn't decided on a date yet, we told them.
"I'll take you to Ireland if you really want" said Rob.
Al leaned across to Rob and kissed him on the lips.
"Thank you" he said looking into Rob's eyes.
It struck me that Rob and Al were so tactile, loving, generous and trusting.
I couldn't quite get my head round the fact that they were so easily able to include ME in their relationship but I figured that was MY problem, not theirs.
I longed to be free enough of my own demons that I might be able to be as loving to Des.
That day seemed a long way off.
I realized that I was the one who had made the first move with Des.
I had seduced him, I suppose, for want of a better way of describing it.
He had fallen for my seduction; he had been seduced.
But I hadn't followed through.
I longed to be more like Al and Rob.
They didn't seem to be held back in the same way that I was.
They weren't held back at all.
They knew what they wanted.
Right now it seemed that I was one of the things they wanted.
Nothing was going to stop them getting what they wanted.

Wasn't it strange then that I wanted Des, but everything was stopping me from getting him?
The biggest thing stopping me from getting him was ME!
Was I afraid of something?

Rob and Al had so much to teach me.
They were afraid of nothing.

There's not a lot more to say about the night of the dinner party.
Once everyone had their fill of food and drink they said their goodbyes and left.
I cleared the table, and Des helped.
We talked as we cleared things away.
"Looks like all our friends are determined we should buy a house together" I said.
"It certainly looks that way" said Des.
"And I know you didn't have a chance to prime them all". I added.
"As if I would do such a thing!" he said with mock surprise.
I stacked everything in the dishwasher and our clean up was finished.
I put the kettle on for a cup of tea for us both.
"Okay" I said, "I'm still not sure it's the best idea in the world but let's look for a house".
"Fantastic" he said "I'll get straight on it, after the weekend".
"The other thing Des" I said.
"Yes".
"The thing with Scout. God help me if I did anything to hurt Scout, and if I did it was an accident I swear. Maybe the vet will find it was from an old injury."
"I told you Charlie, I believe you" he said.
"Well, if you believe me then that's okay. But I was hoping we could keep Scout, and maybe if he becomes too much of a handful my parents can look after him occasionally".
"Don't worry Charlie, we'll work something out".

I felt I was leaving out huge chunks; things that needed to be said but that I'd forgotten.
I felt I could never tell Des what had happened between Rob, Al and me, in our bedroom.
No it wasn't that.
There was something else.
What was it?

"I know that you cut yourself today, Charlie. I saw the kitchen towels and the knife. And the bandage! Do you want to talk about it?"

Bang! There it was.

The truth was that I didn't want to talk about it, ever.
As far as I was concerned I'd been careless and left the knife and kitchen towels out where Des could see them.
Beyond that there was nothing I wanted to contemplate.
Even so I recognised that Des needed to hear what I had to say.
I loved him enough that I should talk to him about the knife, the cutting.

I sat down with my tea, and Des followed suit.

I decided to start at the beginning.

"I know that I've been totally stressed out Des, what with work and everything. Then I felt I was being pressured to move in with you. Then to top it all it felt like you didn't believe me about Scout".
"But I DO believe you" he said.

"The point is that I didn't feel you believed me. Then you left to go to the vet. I was left here alone driving myself MAD with frustration, and hurt and pain. I really didn't know what to do about it. I couldn't play piano, or sit quietly, or read, or anything. I felt myself spiralling downwards, and then I finally remembered something that used to work for me".

"Cutting yourself?" He said quietly.

"Yes, cutting myself. I used to cut myself, I told you, when I was a lot younger. It's not something I'm proud of, but it seemed to work. It stopped me going mad".

We sat quietly for a minute.

"I'll tell you this" I added. "When I STOPPED cutting myself was when I went down my darkest and deepest hole. That was when I stopped talking, stopped moving altogether".

Des just held my hand and let me continue talking.

"I don't know if that makes any sense to you at all?" I said.

"All I can think of is that the place you were escaping to sounds pretty bad, so the place you were escaping from had to be a hell of a lot worse" he said. "Do you want to talk about that?"

"I'm not sure if I can."

Even so I thought I owed it to Des to try.

"My mother has never been very motherly, and one day you'll know what I'm talking about, because you'll meet her. She really had no time for me when I was growing up. I don't remember a time when she showed any love or affection towards me. When I say it out loud it doesn't sound so bad, does it? 'She didn't show any love or affection', big deal, get over it. Jim Watson should have been the person who could bring love and affection into my life. One weekend, when I was about five, he took us to the seaside. I needed to use the toilet and he took me into the cubicle. That's how it all started. I thought it was all part of what a daddy does. He wasn't particularly violent, as such. I didn't like being buggered by him, but I was only small and he was a very big man. So of course I wouldn't like being buggered. The thing is that I don't hate the man. Maybe I should. If I hate anyone it's myself. Second on the list is my mother because she conditioned me to accept Jim's advances. She didn't know she was doing it. But she was doing it nonetheless. Every time she pushed me away instead of giving me a goodnight kiss, every time she screamed at me to finish a chore. I was more useful to her as a servant, that's how I felt. Dad showed me affection, although I know now it was the wrong affection".

This was the most I'd ever talked about it.

"Then Dad's advances became more insistent, and the situations we found ourselves in more risky. I found myself becoming two different people; one was the small innocent boy, the other was the devious, deceitful deviant. I splintered my personality in two, or that's the way it felt. I know I should have told someone, but who? I couldn't tell my mother because she wouldn't have believed me. There was no one else. It felt like Dad was the only one in the world I could speak to. He warned me not to tell anyone else, because no one would believe me. He said that if I told anyone then I might never see him again. He asked me 'did I want that?'. Wasn't he the one who loved me more than anyone else in the world? The weirdest thing is, that he probably did love me more than anyone else. Yes it was the wrong kind of love, but believe me, when you're a kid and you don't get the right kind of love, then the wrong kind of love will do."

Des squeezed my hand gently.

"Go on" he said, "I want to know it all"

"I don't know. You pretty much know it all now."

"When did you start cutting?" he asked.

"Well, the thing is there was no escape. My mother was happy for Jim to be the main parent. So he would bathe me, dress me, drive me to and from school, take me to football, and swimming. He'd wake me in the mornings and put me to bed every night. Wherever he took me, whatever we did together, he would touch, caress, play with me. Whatever you want to call it. There were many times we were nearly caught. Then, one time, we WERE caught. We were on a train going somewhere, in an empty single compartment. The train was pulling into a station as Dad made me suck him. Dad wasn't expecting an old lady to swing the door open just as he was coming. It was disgusting. I was about twelve. The innocent Charlie was doing battle with deviant Charlie. I started cutting then. Cutting myself seemed to quiet both voices"

I was finished for now.

Then Des asked me something unexpected.

"How did Duffy come into you life?"

"Jim decided one day that he was going to take me to the dog home to pick up a rescue puppy, and we chose Duffy".

"That's it? That's all?" asked Des.

"I guess Duffy might have been some kind of reward, I don't know. Dad was driving us in his red Jaguar. Anyway, I remember that on the drive home Jim wanted to stop off somewhere for the usual" I answered.

"The usual what?"

"The usual wank, or blowjob or fuck" I said. "Sorry to be so crude, but that's what it was".

"That's okay" he said. "And how old would you have been then?"

"About seven I guess".

"And when did you start playing piano?"

"What IS this Des? Therapy?"

"If you like. I'd just like to know."

"I guess I was seven when I started playing piano".

"How did that happen?"

"Oh, I don't know. We inherited an old upright piano, and I would tinkle away on it. I guess someone, probably Jim, thought I might have some talent".

"Well you DO have a talent, that's for sure. Even so it sounds like Jim was very cleverly rewarding you, leading you wherever he wanted you to go. I'm not a therapist, but that's the way it seems to me. I think it might really help you if you were to see a professional" he said.

"Believe me Des, I think I've seen enough professionals." Des had his arm round me now.

"Did you talk to any of these professionals about Jim?" I had to think.

"I don't think I did". I admitted.

"So none of these professionals ever got to the root of your breakdown?" he asked.

""Well I wasn't about to tell them, was I?"

"So what did these professionals do to help you heal?" he asked me.

"Well, music therapy helped a lot I guess, counselling sessions, group therapy. That kind of thing."

"And in these counselling sessions, what did these professionals think was the matter with you?"

"I guess they thought I'd just cracked under the pressure of school" I said.

"Because you never told them the truth?"

"Well, yes" I said.

"Charlie, how many people know what happened between you and Jim Watson?"

I thought for a second.

"Well there's me, Jim Watson, my mother, and now you! Oh and that little old lady at the train station".

"The little old lady doesn't count" smiled Des. "Though I'd say it was a bit of a shock for her".

It was getting very late. I had a busy day tomorrow as usual.

"What about Scout?" I asked.

"I should be able to pick him up after I drop you off at Mrs Van Nord's house!.

"That would be good, thanks" I said.

"As for Jim, and cutting yourself, we haven't finished talking about that. Don't worry though" he said. "We'll go at any speed you want. We'll fix this Charlie. That's my promise."

I was earning about a hundred dollars a week teaching Mrs Van Nord's students.

I decided that I should visit her in the hospital.

Des agreed to come with me.

The first time I'd met her I saw a slim woman of average height with Nordic features and colouring, aged about sixty.

She smelled of lavender.

This time she was noticeably more gaunt.

She was skeletal, but still smelling of lavender.

Des and I came into her room, shown in by a nurse.

Mrs Van Nord was lying on her hospital bed, hooked up to morphine and a saline drip.

The pale skin of her arms had the texture of brown paper, and I could see the veins beneath it pulsing weakly.

She smiled at me.

I hope she recognized me, but I think she was on a LOT of morphine, so I can only hope.

I tried to be jolly, smiled warmly at her.

Des stood in the background.

I held her hand.

I explained who Des was, and she nodded vaguely.

Her eyes sparkled, and I thought I could see a joyful intelligence at play there, but I may have seen it wrong.

There wasn't a lot I could say except to tell her how her individual students were doing.

By now I knew all of them by name, as Mrs Van Nord would have done.

Jamie with the Bach minuet, Tammy with Le Coucou, Robin with the Field nocturne. I told her they were all doing well, but that they missed her and always asked after her, which was true.

I think I knew instinctively that I would never see Mrs Van Nord again.

I didn't know her well enough for it to be a sad realization.

Instead I saw it all as part of the cycle of life and death.

She seemed to me to be more like an angel than anything else, even though she was ancient looking and immobile.

This ethereal quality was coming mostly from her eyes.

"Goodbye, Mrs Van Nord" I said.

There were tears in my eyes now and I kissed her gently on her forehead.

We left her there.

We were very quiet as we drove home.

Scout's injury; the results were inconclusive.
The vet couldn't tell for sure if it was an old injury made
worse, (by me), or a new one, (probably caused by me).
I was neither innocent nor guilty, but I was acquitted
through lack of evidence.
Scout wore a cast which had to stay on for the next couple
of months.

I moved out of the apartment above Reds Bar, and into
Des's place.
We started looking for a house; something big enough for
the two of us and Scout. We worked together with an
estate agent who, once a week, would present us with a
booklet.
The estate agent's booklet contained details and pictures of
houses we might find suitable.
We set aside a few hours once a week to search for a place.

It was nearly time for the end of year recital.
I had to perform the Kabalevsky, all three movements, in
front of a packed auditorium.
This would make up my credits for the first year.
I was ready, I thought.
The thing was that every time I played the sonata in its
entirety I was thoroughly emotionally drained.
Of course I had to play it every day, and this had a huge
negative psychic effect.
Miss Clokovsky was back to her fierce and economical
self.
I was never praised again, not in the way she'd praised my
slow Beethoven.

Des had an opera to finish and he had nearly done it.

He only had the last part to finish, which he called 'the Submariners' Sarabande'.
As soon as it was finished he would have all the individual orchestral parts copied, and then rehearsals could be organized.

So far I had yet to meet Sandra, Des's wife.
I still hadn't met his son Nicholas.
I wasn't going to push Des into organizing a meeting.
It wasn't the kind of thing that either of us looked forward to.
Even so, we would have to bite the bullet at some time, and soon.

It looked like we could see a natural gap coming up when we could take a trip to Ireland.
The only problem was going to be finding a replacement organist while I was away. The only way to find a solution was to have a chat with Bette about it.
This meant there would be a likelihood that Des would finally meet Riff and my mother.
Riff was now back from his sea trip.
I couldn't keep Des and my mother separated forever, (could I?), so a meeting was inevitable.
I didn't tell Des very much about what my mother was like.
I thought it best that he find out for himself.
Somehow it was arranged that Des and I would have Sunday lunch with Bette, Riff and my mother.
I really didn't like the idea.
I much preferred keeping all the different parts of my life compartmentalised.
I had a terrible feeling of dread, as if everything was about to cascade around me.

Suddenly I was in a position where I didn't have to find three hundred dollars extra a month for the rent on the Reds apartment.

I was able to quit one of my jobs.

I handed in my notice at the Fisherman's Rest.

Barb was very upset about this.

I was no longer going to be her flat mate, and neither was I going to be her work mate.

She decided to throw me a surprise party.

Of course I knew nothing about it until the night Des took me to the Reds apartment, (my old apartment), some time in May or June.

I had thought we were just popping round there to say a quick hello before visiting the bar downstairs; Reds, my old haunt.

We stood outside of my old apartment and rang the bell.

Barb came to the door, an enormous smile on her face, and her arms thrown open to greet us. Her long strawberry blonde hair was loose. She wore an Indian print smock tied about the waist with multicoloured braid, and golden sandals on her pedicured feet.

"Come in, come in, stranger" she said to me, guiding me through to the front room. There was a lot of noise, subdued chatter, Miles Davis on the stereo.

When I was shown into the front room there was a loud and sudden cheer.

Everyone I knew, virtually, was in that room.

Roger threw an arm around my shoulder and gave me a beer.

Mick passed me a joint, (of course).

Rob and Al were nearby, grinning at me mischievously.

Who knew what they were planning tonight?

"It's sort of the opposite of a house warming. Combined with your farewell party from the Fisherman's" Barb explained.

"Oh Barb, you angel, I don't deserve this" I said.

I felt a little bit uncomfortable, but I appreciated the thought that had gone behind it.

"I'm going to miss living with you," she said, "and working with you".

"Mick has a whole room for his plants now" I said. "His grass can spread out of my cupboard now".

"Like triffids?" she said, and I laughed.

"I know it sounds strange Barb, but can I have one last look at my old room?" I asked her.

"Of course" she said.

She took me by the hand and I followed her to my old room.

The big double bed was made up with fresh white linen, there were candles flickering in every nook.

It looked magical.

I had a library of wonderful memories attached to this room, and I felt quite emotional.

"It's okay Charlie" said Barb, and she pulled me towards her, and we hugged.

She had her hand in my hair and was stroking me there.

She gently pulled my face towards her and kissed me.

It was a deep and sensual kiss, and I found myself returning it without really meaning to.

She let go of me, saying "I've always wanted to do that".

"Really?" I asked her.

"Sure! Didn't you know?"

I was very fond of Barb, but I had never had the slightest inkling that she might have longed to kiss me.

It touched me, and it confused me.

I felt that I must be going through life wearing some sort of blindfold.

"We should go and join the party. It's YOUR party after all" she said.

'So What' was playing on the stereo.

Mick came over to me, "Thanks buddy" he said. "Letting me use your cupboard like that".

"No problem Mick" I said. "Let's hope the new flat mate let's you carry on using it".

"No" he said. "This is the end of an era. Me and Ursie are heading to Europe for the summer, and then who knows where?"

"No! Why?"

"We've had it with this town. Small people with small minds and small lives".

"Oh Mick, we're not all like that!" I said.

"You're not from here. You don't count".

"Thanks, I think", I laughed.

So if I had now moved out of the apartment, and Mick and Ursie were leaving, then that left only Roger, Barb and Mark.

I wondered what would happen to them now.

I knew that I wasn't the cause of this 'end of an era' as Mick put it.

But I was part of it.

Somehow that made me feel responsible, ridiculous as that might sound.

Ursie Passion Flower came over to me and gave me a big hug.

She had short curly hair, and was built like a shot putter.

I know I haven't said much about my flat mates but I was fond of them all.

"Did you hear?" she asked.

"No, what?" I replied.

"You left at exactly the right time. They're going to knock down this whole building. No more Reds! No more apartment"

I couldn't believe it.

"I heard you're heading for Europe" I said.

"Yeah. Can't wait to leave hicksville I can tell you"

"Oh Ursie, I'll be so sorry to see you both go".

"I know, what can you do?"

"We'll keep in touch though?" I said.

"Sure" she said, and I knew from the tone of her voice that we'd probably never see each other again.

Des was in conversation with Al and Rob.

I left them to it.

I found Roger in the kitchen.

"Did you hear?" he asked. "they're knocking the place down".

"I heard. What are you going to do?" I asked.

"I'll go home to my folks place for the summer, then I'll find a place when I come back for the second year".

"That sounds easy enough, eh?" I asked him.

"It'll all work out. It always does. Maybe I'll get lucky like you, and find me a sugar daddy", he laughed.

I knew he didn't really see Des as my sugar daddy.

At least I hoped he didn't see Des that way.

"You tried being gay, for a night, remember? That didn't work out! You didn't like it! Remember now?"

"Oh yes," he chuckled. "A sugar mummy then, if there's such a thing".

I had a sudden flash of an idea. I needed to speak to Des about it.

I could suggest that our new house could be bigger than we really needed, and that we could have Roger as a lodger. 'Roger the lodger' I thought to myself, and laughed to myself quietly.

"What are you laughing at?" Roger asked.

"I just had an idea" and I told him.

"Roger the lodger, I could deal with that!"

I promised to talk to Des about it.

"You have till September to make it all happen buddy".

Barb and her boyfriend, Mark, had bought a couple of bottles of tequila.

The party had got a lot rowdier now as a result.

Roger and I were still in the kitchen when Mark came into us with the second tequila bottle and a couple of shot glasses.

He was completely naked.

He was built like a chubby weightlifter.

"What the fuck's happening now?" Roger exclaimed, shaking his head, laughing.

"Nothin', we just decided we're havin' us a nekkid party" he said matter-of-factly.

"Oh is that all?" Roger said.

Then to me he said "Are you up for this?"

I downed a shot of tequila and said "Why the hell not?"

We got all our clothes off.

"Can I leave these in your room?" I asked Roger, indicating my pile of clothing.

"Sure, that's what I'm gonna do".

We dumped our clothes and then rejoined the party.

There was a huge cheer as we entered the room.
Sure enough, everyone else in the room was naked as the day they were born, all except Des.
He still had on his tie, but nothing else.
He had found himself the best chair and seemed to be holding court.
Everyone was around him, listening rapt, as he told one of his wonderful stories.

Dieter, the German neighbour from across the hall, was talking to me.
His command of the English language wasn't exactly comprehensible, and talking with him was difficult sometimes.
Tonight however, fuelled by tequila and nakedness, conversation was somehow made easier.
Dieter worked as the chef in Reds bar, downstairs.
It occurred to me that he'd soon be without a job and without a home.
I decided tonight might not be the night to bring that up.
We were having one hell of a party and I wasn't going to be the one to dampen the mood.
"You" he said. "You are like the piece of paper. You rip yourself into little pieces. Then you leave a trail, with hope that someone will find you!.
"Do I?" I was intrigued.
"They sniff after you like dogs" he said.
"Who are you talking about?"
"Everybody" he said laughing. "Everybody" and he waved his arm around the room not indicating anyone in particular.
"Is that a good thing?" I asked.

"It depends" he looked at me with beady eyes. "Is it good for you? I don't know. Is it good for the dogs? No, it is never good for the dogs" and he laughed like a maniac.

I still wasn't sure what he meant.

I was convinced that HE knew what he meant though.

Dieter was a big lump of a man, and his large body was covered in thick black hair. Right now he was spitting with every word he spoke.

I felt momentarily trapped.

I looked around to see if anyone might rescue me.

I knew Dieter only vaguely.

He'd been in our apartment on many occasions but I was always on my way out, busy with my various jobs.

I had eaten food he'd prepared in Reds' kitchen on many occasions.

 He wasn't a bad chef.

The last time he cooked he had decided he was going to make escargots.

I couldn't bring myself to taste that particular dish, and I think he held that against me.

"But one day," Dieter added. "One day the dogs will find you".

He was looking me straight in the eye, almost angrily.

"And when they find you, my friend, they will put all those little pieces of paper back together. And THEN they will know, we will ALL know, who you really are!"

I was feeling really threatened by Dieter now.

Years of conditioning had taught me that the best way of dealing with a threat was to ride it out, and be polite.

I think it's also the English way.

Dieter, I knew, wasn't going to physically threaten me.

But it seemed that he had something worse than physical threat planned for me.

"And what do you think the dogs will discover Dieter?" I asked, putting my clipped English accent to best use, trying to intimidate him with it, as he was intimidating me. It didn't work.

He moved very close to me, menacingly.

"The dogs will discover the thing you hide" he whispered. "They will see that the little pieces of paper you leave as a trail mean nothing. They will put all the pieces of paper back together, and they will see only a blank page. They will discover, my friend, that you are really nothing. Only the trail you leave. And even the trail is nothing!"

It seemed obvious to me now that Dieter had developed a deep dislike of me, and I couldn't figure out why.

Surely it wasn't because I hadn't eaten his escargots?

"But we are all friends here tonight, ja?" and his tone changed back to that of a jolly German. "It is your party. Enjoy it".

I felt a warm hand on my bare shoulder.

Thankfully someone had come to rescue me.

It was Rob, my favourite cellar-man.

"I need you to come with me" he said.

I felt like I was in a spy movie.

It didn't fell like real life, that was certain.

"Where are we going?" I asked.

"You'll see" he said.

He took my hand and I followed him.

We were now in my old bedroom, with fresh white linen and candles.

He closed the door behind us.

He picked me up, easily, in his strong arms and threw me on the bed.

"Rob, don't do this" I begged.

"Shh" he said. "Don't worry everything's going to be just fine".

I couldn't see how anything was going to be 'just fine'.

He pushed me down and got on top of me, straddled me like a cowboy riding his horse.

The door handle turned and my heart leapt at the prospect of discovery.

It was Al, and immediately behind him was Des, still wearing his tie, and carrying a glass of wine.

'What now?' I thought.

Al guided Des to the bed and made him lie down next to me.

Then Al straddled Des.

Des turned to me, then kissed me, not saying a word.

He grabbed a hold of my hand.

We both surrendered to the will of our captors, our seducers.

Rob and Al rocked back and forth until Des and I were both erect.

Then at some unseen signal Al and Rob grabbed our legs and doubled us nearly in two so that our butt cheeks were closest to Rob and Al's faces.

Then Rob and Al began to lick our butt cheeks and holes. It was delicious, indescribably delicious.

I could hear Des moan, and found that my moaning was almost in sync with his.

Rob and Al must have somehow decided to be sexual mirrors, or copies of each other. I don't know when they could have decided it. Or how any of this had been arranged between them.

It didn't matter.

Rob spent a long time relaxing me, relaxing my hole.

When I was fully relaxed he shifted my body again, and suddenly he was inside me. I'd been buggered before, but it had never been like this.

In the past it had only ever been agony.

Now it was the opposite.

It was purest ecstasy.

I was vaguely aware that Al was now doing the exact same thing to Des.

Rob was fucking me, but a different hand was wanking me.

It was Al's hand.

At the same time, and with the same motion, Rob was wanking Dennis.

I felt Dennis's hand squeeze mine more tightly. He turned slightly so as to kiss me, and with that we both came.

Rob and Al came at the same time too, inside us.

It was a simultaneous quadruple orgasm.

There was a knock on the door.

The door opened.

It was Roger.

He said "Sorry" and closed the door.

All four of us burst into spontaneous laughter.

Then we all lay there together in a chaotic heap, cuddling and kissing.

"Oh my" said Des.

I felt like I was glowing; a slight sweat over every inch of me.

I could see the same glow of sweat coming from Rob, Al and Des.

We got cleaned up, by visiting the bathroom one at a time.

Des went first.

I was alone with Rob and Al now.

I felt I had to ask something, but didn't want to ruin the moment.

"Have you guys been planning this?"

Rob and Al looked at each other.

Al answered.

"Right from the start" he said.

"Oh" I said.

It seemed to answer everything I needed right now.

We carried on hugging and kissing until Des came back.

Rob went to use the bathroom.

Des had a question.

"Do you guys do this all the time?" he asked.

"Don't ask me" I told him.

"I was asking Al".

"Not very often. Sometimes." He said.

Rob returned and Al used the bathroom.

"That's the problem with an orgy" said Rob. "You don't know who to thank" and we all laughed then, and any tension we might have felt was dissipated.

Trust Rob to do that!

Al came back into the room and it was my turn to clean up.

It only took a minute or at most two.

When I got back to my old bedroom we decided to rejoin the naked party which was still in full swing.

'You Can Ring My Bell' was now being played on the stereo, and a few naked bodies were dancing.

I realized that our little group of four was now inseparable.

I didn't know how long we'd be like that, but it lasted for the rest of the night at least.

Roger sidled up to me.

"Des will have trouble getting back into his closet now" he said.

"Why's that?" I asked.
"He just broke all the doors getting out!"

I was drunk with tequila and beer. I was stoned on Mick's grass.
All I really wanted to do was go to bed.
With Des.
Maybe with Al and Rob too.
The problem was that we now had a puppy.
The other problem was that I had another busy day.
I needed to be home.
Home was now with Des, in his apartment.
Our apartment.

We got home very late to discover that Scout had eaten every single shoe in the place.
Des was uncharacteristically angry.
"Relax" I said. "He's a puppy, and that's what puppies do. He'll grow out of it".

We went straight to bed.
Scout joined us.
We chatted a little before dropping off to sleep.
 Maybe it might seem like a surprise that we didn't analyse our little foursome! Anyway, we didn't.
"They're knocking down Reds" I said.
"I heard".
"I have an idea" I said.
"I'm listening".
"How about we find a slightly larger house than we need and have Roger rent a room off us."
"Brilliant idea" he said.
He chuckled.
"Roger the lodger!" he said.

I chuckled too.

That was all the discussion we needed.

Soon we'd be looking for a house big enough to home us, Scout and Roger the lodger.

"By the way Charlie" he added. "That was something wasn't it?"

I knew he was talking about our foursome.

"It sure was Doc".

We started looking for a four bedroom house close to the university.

There were several within our budget.

It needed to have an enclosed yard so Scout would be safe. This narrowed it down.

In the end we found a house that might be suitable.

Des drove us to the place and parked in the drive.

"You have to learn how to drive, Charlie. I can't always be chauffeur".

He was right and I relished the idea.

"I'll teach you if you like".

I had visions of us stopping off somewhere, during my driving lesson, and doing things together that we shouldn't!

The estate agent knocked on the window.

Then he showed us round the place.

It had the enclosed yard we were looking for.

It was a wood-clad house built, in the twenties, that overlooked the harbour.

It had all its original period features, but that included the original furnace and wiring. It would need some work.

It had four big bedrooms.

It was a five minute walk from the university, and five minutes the other way would take you to Rob and Al's house.

It was ten minutes walk from Harold's House.

If it's all about location then this was the perfect place.

Des told me that his son could walk here from the marital home.

I hadn't even thought of this.

Of course he would want his son to visit!

We looked at the reception rooms.

There was a large kitchen and even a scullery!

We looked at all the bedrooms and the view from each window was spectacular.

Outside there was a garage-come-workshop, with a floor above that might be space for a guest house.

I was trying to conceal my excitement but I was in love with this house.

It seemed that Des had also fallen in love with it.

Des had figured out that if we had a lodger we could afford a bigger and better place. We could afford this place!

We made an offer.

It was accepted.

We were first time buyers and not part of a chain.

The vendors had already vacated the property.

Once our mortgage application had been accepted and all the papers signed we could move in.

It might take only a few weeks.

One of the papers that we had to sign was concerned with insurance.

Ours would be a joint mortgage and the only way to finalise it would be with proper insurance.

The policy we signed said that, in the event of one of us dying, the property would be completely paid for, and that a substantial amount would be paid out to the survivor.

It all seemed a bit morbid to me, but we signed anyway.

There was one clause which stated that the policy was void in cases of suicide.

I didn't plan on suicide.

I was sure Des wasn't thinking of it either.

Des thought of booking a kennel for Scout so we could travel to Ireland, (probably at the end of August or the beginning of September).

I hated the idea of putting Scout into a kennel when he was so young.

Then a thought came to me.

I thought the time had come that I should introduce Des to my family.

Then maybe we could get Riff and my mother to look after Scout while we were away.

Obviously my mother, and Riff, knew about Des.

They hadn't yet met him.

They didn't know that he was my lover and my partner.

I was heading for the moment I dreaded.

The moment when it all cascaded around me.

If you've ever owned a puppy you know they require patience and a lot of discipline. I had the patience but none of the discipline. Des, it turned out, had both.

I made it my job to clear up any puppy mess, whether it be chewed clothes or shoes, or his shit and piss.

The apartment was not a great place to raise a puppy.

We needed to be in the new house as soon as we possibly could, if only for the sake of Scout, and our sanity.

Des was making phone calls to Ireland, speaking to his aunt, I guessed, to arrange our trip.

I had told Mrs Van Nord's students that I would soon have my own place, with a grand piano. I said I was closing down Mrs Van Nord's house for the summer, but that in the new term we'd begin again in a new location. This suited most of them fine. Only two thought it was too far a journey to make, just for a piano lesson, and I lost them as students.

Des was with me in church while I played my regular Sunday gig.
Bette gave a brilliant sermon, as usual, this time about faith in adversity.
My mother and Riff also sat in the congregation.
I knew that everything would be fine just as long as the service was in progress.
I was more worried about what might come after.
Better had invited the family to Sunday lunch at her house, directly opposite the church.
At the end of the service Bette's custom was to shake the hand of her parishioners as they left, at the front door of her church.
I remember her always smiling.
I didn't know her well enough to be able to say that I loved her.
What I felt for her was a warmth and fondness that has nothing to do with how WELL I knew her.
She made me feel good about myself.
She made everyone feel that way. That was her gift.

"Charlie. Des" she said. "Now, the house is open. Just go over and let yourselves in. Make yourselves at home."
I could see that Bette had the same effect on Des as she had on me.
He was instantly at ease with her.

I could see my mother and Riff behind us now, in the queue to leave the church.

We left them behind us, in the queue, and crossed the road to Bette's white painted bungalow, with the picket fence.

Her house had a view of the sea.

Bette's dining room window looked onto the waves as they crashed onto the stony shore.

It was a beautiful day.

Her table was already set, with napkins, fine cutlery and crystal glasses.

There was a vase of white flowers as the centrepiece.

The smell of a Sunday roast filled the air.

"This is very civilized" said Des admiringly.

It amazed me, every time, that Bette managed to prepare a Sunday roast every Sunday and simultaneously prepare for her service.

Riff and my mother were letting themselves in through the front door.

I heard Riff's voice before I saw him.

"Something smells good" he said.

"Anybody home?" said my mother's sweet, sing-song voice.

"We're in here" I half shouted.

"Hi, Charlie" said Riff, extending a hand to me in greeting.

He had a good strong handshake.

"Hi Riff, how are you?"

"Couldn't be better" he said. "And who is this?"

"This" I said "is Des"

"Oh, you're Charlie's professor at university aren't you?" my mother asked.

My mother has a wide variety of voices that she uses.

She has one for every occasion.

Right now she used her absolutely best accent.

It was like her best china; only used on the most important of occasions.

"I'm a doctor" he said. "A doctor of music".

"Oh dear" she said. "Is it ill?"

"Is what ill?" I interjected.

"Music, dear. Is that why it needs a doctor?"

Riff was amused.

He had inherited Bette's bright blue eyes, and they sparkled now.

"Forget it Des" he said. "You've lost this round".

My mother had the look of an innocent child, unaware she might have said anything amusing.

"Mum" I said. "Des just bought a new house."

"That's wonderful" she said.

"He asked me to share with him".

"Oh that's wonderful. It will help with your bills. And Charlie will make a good lodger, if he ever learns to tidy up after himself".

This was going to be easier, in a way, than I imagined.

"The struggles I had with him when he was growing up" she sighed, "I can tell you".

"Dianne" said Riff, "probably not a good time".

"What are you talking about? I'm sure Des would love to hear what he's getting into with Charlie here."

"I'm quite sure he wouldn't" Riff objected.

Bette came in through the front door, just in time.

"That's my sheep sorted for the week" she said, with a grin.

"Mother" said Riff. "I have some booze in the car".

"Perfect darling" she said.

To Des he said "Can you give me a hand?"

"Surely" replied Des.

"He seems very nice" said my mother, in her slightly less shiny voice.

"He really is" I told her.

I was in no doubt that Riff was apologising to Des at this very minute.

"I hope everyone is happy with roast beef" announced Bette from her kitchen.

"Do you need a hand Mrs Rifkind?" asked my mother.

I don't know why my mother called her that.

Everyone else called her 'Bette'.

The interesting thing, to me, was that my mother's name was 'Mrs Rifkind' now too.

"I keep telling you to call me Bette, dear."

"I know, but it just won't stick somehow" my mother explained.

"At least you don't call me Reverend, so I suppose that's something" Bette said in a lower tone. "Anyway, it's all under control".

With that Bette brought a silver platter of roast beef into the dining room.

"Please be seated everyone" she said. "Oh" she added, when she saw that Des and Riff were still outside.

At that second there was a bustle at the front door, Riff chatting easily to Des, as they carried drink into the kitchen.

Soon we were all seated around the table.

Bette grabbed the hands of Riff and Des, who were sat either side of her."

"I hope it doesn't offend you Des, but we say Grace in this house" Bette said.

"Not at all" he said.

"Would you like to say Grace Charlie?" she asked me.
I held Des's hand, and my mother's.
We all bowed our heads.
"Thank you for the gifts You have given us. Bless everyone around this table, and everyone who is in our lives. Bless those less fortunate than we are. Bless our absent loved ones, wherever they are, in Heaven or on Earth".
"Amen" said Bette. "That was lovely Charlie, thank you".
I grinned at her.
Bette served food and Riff made sure every glass was filled.

Eventually there was enough gap in the conversation that I could bring up the subject of Scout.
"The thing is that Des now has a puppy, called Scout".
"Oh lovely" said my mother in her best voice. "What breed?"
"A black Labrador".
"Oh, like Duffy?" she said.
"Like Duffy, only a puppy. Anyway, with all the stuff going on at the new house Des wanted to put Scout into a kennel. Just for two weeks."
"Well that won't do" said Riff. "We would happily look after Scout till the house is ready".
"Oh I couldn't..." Des trailed off. I knew he was being polite.
"Nonsense. It would be unfair on the pup to put him in a strange kennel" said Riff.
Our mission had been accomplished, as easy as that.
My mother chose this moment to tell everyone about the day that Duffy died, but more specifically about my premonition.

"Charlie told me to look after the dogs. He'd just had this awful dream, didn't you Charlie? And then, within hours Duffy had been run over. It was a premonition. Charlie has a gift" she finished with a flourish.

"I didn't know any of this" said Des with interest.

By the way he was looking at me I could tell he was expecting a response.

In fact everyone was looking at me now.

"Do you know what I think?" asked Bette.

There was an expectant silence, so she continued.

"There are times when something so terrible happens that it sends out ripples; ripples of distress and dread. I don't see any reason why those ripples shouldn't be able to travel into the past just as easily as they travel into the future."

"Well put mother" said Riff.

"I try David, thank you" she smiled warmly at him.

I wished my mother would smile at me as warmly and as genuinely.

"Well I think he has a gift" my mother cut in dismissively.

"He got that from me, didn't you Charlie?"

"I didn't know you had premonitions" said Riff, with a slight edge of disbelief.

"Oh yes, darling. All the time." She was cat-like now. "I don't tell you EVERYTHING".

I knew instinctively from my mother's tone that an embarrassing scene might erupt. Riff remained silent, with his head down, contemplating his next mouthful of food.

"I believe a husband and wife should HAVE no secrets" said Bette.

"We're not ALL perfect" said my mother. Her body had stiffened as if she was ready for a fight.

I could see Des was confused about this hidden undercurrent.

He decided to come to the rescue.

"Have you had other premonitions Charlie" he asked me.

"No, not that I remember" I told him.

"Oh that reminds me" said my mother nonchalantly.

"There was a call this morning".

She had our attention.

"It was Peter Van Nord, Mrs Van Nord's son. He just wanted to let us know that his mother passed away in the early hours this morning".

I'm so used to my mother that I'm rarely shocked by her. On this occasion I could see the shock on every other face around the table.

My mother wanted so badly to be the centre of attention that she would do or say anything.

She had no boundaries.

She found it completely acceptable to serve this piece of news at Bette's dinner table.

Bette found her voice first.

"I'm so sorry to hear that" she said. "I never met her but I understand she was a lovely spirited woman. I heard she was very ill."

Bette knew Mrs Van Nord was ill because I had told her. Mrs Van Nord's illness was the reason I taught piano every Saturday.

My mother ignored Bette.

She was like an out of control steam roller.

"Peter, the son, is coming up from California to look after her affairs. He's an actor, you know, and very handsome so I hear". She said this in such a way that I knew it was aimed at Riff.

There was no stopping her now.

"Of course, Mrs Van Nord was so grateful to you, Charlie, that she left you her piano. Isn't that wonderful?"

I was still stunned by the news of Mrs Van Nord's death
that I felt I was on automatic pilot.
"Yes, that's wonderful" I agreed.
"Well, when Peter comes up from California you can have
a little chat with him and get the piano".
"We already have a piano" said Des, and he saw me
shaking my head at him.
My mother pursed her lips.
"WE?" she said.
"Yes" I cut in. "We have a piano in the house. A big black
grand piano".
"Well, if you don't WANT Mrs Van Nord's piano, after all
she's done for you, then I'm sure she wouldn't mind you
selling it. It can go towards your school fees!"
"Yes" I said. "I suppose I could do that".
"Anyway, my point is" she said "that I had a premonition
that Mrs Van Nord was going to die."
"We ALL knew Mrs Van Nord was going to die" said
Riff. "She had terminal cancer Dianne!"
"No! No! No! Before that. Before she went into hospital!"
"Well you never said" Riff countered.
"As I said; I don't tell you EVERYTHING!"
"That explains it Charlie" Bette said with some
amusement. "You inherited your mother's gift".
"That's what I was trying to tell you" said my mother.
With that my mother ploughed into her meal as if she
hadn't eaten in a week.

Chapter Four

"What an interesting family you have Charlie" said Doc.
We were heading home to the apartment.

The car had learner plates on the front and back these days because Doc was teaching me how to drive.

I discovered that he wasn't just a brilliant Music teacher. He was a great driving instructor too.

I was completely certain he was just one of life's great natural teachers, regardless of the subject.

I was at the wheel.

I loved driving now.

"When you say 'interesting' do you really mean 'nightmarish'?"

"Well I thought Bette and Riff were really down-to-earth. And your mother, Dianne, is definitely in a league of her own" he said.

"At least we have Scout sorted out now. Whatever else she may be my mother is good with animals" I told him.

"I think we did pretty well back there" he said. "There were one or two tricky moments, but we got through it all, pretty much unscathed".

"I'm not 'unscathed'. I'm still in shock about Mrs Van Nord" I said.

"I know, I know" he said with care.

"What was worse, in a way, was how my mother just announced it, as if it was, I don't know, a bring and buy sale!"

"You mustn't let her get to you" he said.

"That's easier said than done Doc" I told him.

I knew Dennis loved my pet name for him. Rob, Al and Roger all called him Doc now.

"What are you going to do about the piano?" he asked me.

"I guess I have to meet up with Peter, the handsome actor" I said.

"Then, for fear of sounding like a jealous husband, I'd better come with you" he told me.

"No, I'm sure it'll be all right".
"Okay, if you're sure".
I told him I was sure.

We had put a child guard in the apartment. It served as a barrier between the kitchen and the rest of the place. Any time that we had to leave Scout alone we'd put him in the kitchen, (with his toys, water, food, and a litter tray), and then close the child guard.
Scout would be out of his cast soon.
He seemed to be getting bigger by the day.
He was boisterous and friendly.
It seemed, now, that he had forgiven me for any injury I might have caused him.
I was thankful for that.
Scout barked his greeting to us as we came in.
My recital was in a few days and I needed to put the finishing touches to the Kabalevsky.
I'd mastered the piece now, but I needed to make it my own.
The first movement was Allegro, but I decided to make it faster, so that it was dangerous and breath-taking.
The second movement I treated as if it was a Chopin Nocturne.
The last movement could be played a number of ways. It could be jagged like a serrated blade, or mathematical as a Bach Fugue. I chose to play it mixing both. I hoped it would work.
The sonata is quite modern, and so the harmonies are unexpected and unbalancing. The minute you think you have something to hold on to, some wisp of a melody or familiar harmony, you're immediately pushed or pulled in a new direction.

It's not a 'nice' piece. It's demanding for performer and listener alike.
I practiced while Doc took Scout for a walk.

I went shopping with Doc and chose a suit for the recital.
It was dark blue, understated but undeniably stylish.
More importantly it was comfortable.
The last thing I needed was to feel restrained by clothing.
All my concentration would be needed for the performance.

On the night of the performance I found myself backstage.
Miss Clokovsky and Doc were with me, as were all the other performers.
I was on first, and I thought this was a good thing because I had less time to be nervous.
It was time.
"How do you feel?" Doc asked me.
"Sick as a dog. And I'm not kidding. I think I'm going to throw up".
Doc laughed.
"You'll be absolutely fine. I know it. Have a good one soldier."
Doc and Miss Clokovsky waited in the wings and, at a signal from the stage manager, I went on stage.
There was warm applause.
I knew that my mother, Riff and Bette would all be in the audience but I couldn't see them because the lights were so bright.
I bowed slightly, as I had been taught, then sat at the stool.
I knew the stool might need adjusting, and turned the handle at the side until it was exactly the right height.
By now the audience was in rapt silence.

I took a deep breath to calm myself.
I mentally scanned through the entire piece to remind myself of difficult landmarks.
I was ready.
I began with a deceptively sweet flourish, taking my audience on a frenzied journey.
The first movement died away. It was partly like it was falling away into the distance, and partly the dying whisper of some mythical animal, a unicorn perhaps.
The second movement was lilting.
It was as if the unicorn was in the underworld now, and longed to be among its own kind once again.
The final movement, and the unicorn could be reborn, but had to go through a terrible baptism of fire.
The journey was at its end now.
I rose from the piano and made a deep bow.
The audience gave me loud and warm applause.
I looked across to the wings, were stood Doc and Miss Clokovsky.
I beckoned to Miss Clokovsky to come on stage with me.
She shook her head but I was insistent.
She came on stage and I took her hand.
She bowed slightly and the applause was louder still.
I wanted her to share the moment.
She looked twenty years younger suddenly.
Her hair, normally iron grey, had turned blonde under the lights.
Her cheeks, which were usually pale and drawn, looked full and rosy.
She was flushed in the reflected glory of her student.
We left the stage together while applause still thundered.
It's very strange but I could smell lavender, and I was reminded of Mrs Van Nord.

I wondered if the recently deceased had the power to visit the ones they left behind on Earth.
In this moment I believed, without a doubt, that they did.

Other students played after me. Among them was Von Chanel. He played Lalo's Symphonie Espagnole. I listened to his performance. He was a virtuoso in my opinion.

Doc was beside me.
"I'm so proud of you" he said, and hugged me tightly.

There was an after recital party, (held in the green room backstage), where all the performers, tutors, family and friends could celebrate the night.
My mother, Riff and Bette were there to congratulate me.
"Of course, you have no idea what a struggle it was to get Charlie to practice. He could be an absolute brat. And his language!" She had turned to Bette. "Oh I can't tell you Mrs Rifkind. He comes across as such a gentleman, but believe me, he was a nasty little shit!"
Riff tried to pull my mother away from his mother, to prevent a scene.
"Dianne, come and say hello to Des" he said.
"Oh, hello Professor" she said in her loveliest voice. "Did you hear Charlie play? Wasn't it wonderful?"
"It certainly was Mrs Rifkind" he said.
"Oh please" she begged. "Call me Dianne".
Riff, thinking he had rescued the situation, thought it might be an idea to get some glasses of punch. I offered to help.
"How's everything Charlie?" he said.
"It's good Riff, thanks" I told him.
I mean, with Des, and the new house and everything?"
"We move in this week" I told him.

"Maybe that's not quite what I meant" he said, and thought of rephrasing.

"What do you mean then?"

"I guess I just have to spit it out. Are you and Des...?"

"You can't make an omelette without breaking eggs" I told him. "Are me and Des what?"

"Are you lovers?" he whispered.

I smiled slightly.

"You should, maybe, think about it before you say anything to your mother" he said.

I said nothing.

I was still basking in the glow of my performance I suppose.

"Well?" he asked. "ARE you lovers?"

"Look Riff" I said. "I have a lot of time for you. I respect you a lot actually. I don't know how you thought Des and I were lovers, (and yes we ARE, but it's NOT common knowledge). One thing is certain though. I have no intention of telling my mother".

"I appreciate it" he said. "It's just I don't need her to have any more ammunition than she already has. It'll just become part of her drama, and I have to deal with the fall-out".

"I DO know what you mean" I told him, nodding.

"Anyway, I guessed. And your grandmother guessed".

I was touched that he thought of his mother as MY grandmother.

"What did she say?" I asked him.

"Listen, it's not like we talk about you behind your back or anything. You know that don't you?"

"I know".

"Anyway, she's absolutely fine with it. She only wants you to be happy. And Des is a good man. She said that herself!"

I thanked him for that.

We took glasses of punch back to our little group.

Riff handed Bette a glass, and one to my mother, who was still in full flow with Des, her captive audience.

"Oh thank you darling" she said as Riff handed her a glass.

I gave Doc his glass of punch which he drank as if it was a magic potion. A potion that might numb my mother's onslaught perhaps.

My mother was not about to be stopped.

She sipped on her punch and then began anew.

"Do you have children professor?" she asked.

"Yes I do, Dianne. I have a son,Nicholas."

"Oh then you know the constant fight, the constant demand for attention. It's always 'me, me, me'. I don't know how one is supposed to care for a demanding child like that and still hold down a job of work".

"What job of work were you doing Dianne?" asked Doc.

"Oh" she said proudly. "I'm a businesswoman!"

"Really" he said with great interest.

"Oh yes, I own several properties. It's very hard work."

"I can only imagine" he said.

I knew Doc well enough now.

My mother wasn't a businesswoman by anyone's definition.

I think Doc knew it.

Admittedly she still owned the house back in England.

When Jim Watson vanished she was left with the house, which she now rented out to pay the mortgage.

It was hardly a full-time job, and it certainly didn't classify her as 'businesswoman of the year.

"You don't know the half of it" she said using her best china voice. "And when you have a young family, well I don't need to tell you."

She paused, took a sip of punch.

"Where is your wife?" she asked Doc.

"We're separated" he explained.

"Ah, how sad! I know how painful that can be. Oh Charlie, I meant to tell you."

She had broken off with Doc to talk to me.

She was like a butterfly in that respect.

"Peter Van Nord will be next door tomorrow, tying up the loose ends, if you want to talk to him about the piano".

"Sure" I said.

"You can bring the professor here for dinner, then you can go and sort out the piano."

"Thank you for inviting me Dianne. I'd love to come to dinner."

"It would be just lovely to have you. I so miss intelligent conversation" she said, and Riff was in earshot.

He joined in at that point.

"I hope you drink scotch Des" he said.

"I've been known to partake on occasion" he replied.

"Good" said Riff. "I have an excellent twelve year old single malt that needs demolishing".

My mother frowned.

"The professor is NOT one of your drinking buddies darling. I'm quite certain he would prefer civilized conversation about music and so on. With ME!"

"That would be delightful" said Doc.

Whatever it was going to be I knew it wasn't going to be delightful.

Riff knew it.

I think Doc knew it too.

Before the evening ended I had a chance to congratulate Von on his performance

"Darling boy" I said. "I adored your Lalo".

I knew I sounded like Noel Coward.

He laughed heartily.

"Thanks Charlie, you put on a good show yourself!" he said, and we patted each other on the back in a masculine hug.

"There's going to be a house warming coming up. Are you game?" I asked him.

"Wouldn't miss it" he said. "Call me, or let Roger know the details."

I promised him I'd do exactly that.

The end of year recital marked the cessation of all study until September.

Most of my days were free now, as they were for Doc.

Doc had stressed to me that we really had to make time to meet his estranged family. He saw his son once a week, but I was never included because I would be a lot to explain away.

I agreed.

I'd finished teaching all Mrs Van Nord's students too.

I would start teaching them all in the new term, but from our new house.

Mrs Van Nord's house was out of bounds anyway, since her death.

Peter Van Nord would most certainly sell the property.

I wondered what he was like.

Was he as handsome as I'd been told?

Doc let me drive his car to my parents house.

I needed very little actual instruction by now, but Doc was free with his encouragement.

I parked in the drive.

I put Scout on his leash and prepared to introduce him to the other dogs.

It would be an event, of that I was sure.

Scout's cast had been taken off and he was more boisterous than ever.

I told Scout to 'sit', and there he sat, on the doorstep, until Riff answered the knock on the door.

"Welcome" he said, and he saw Scout.

"And this must be Scout. How are you little buddy?"

Riff was on his haunches, petting Scout.

Scout was ecstatic at all the attention.

We entered the house.

Riff said he'd let all the dogs introduce themselves to each other, and there were ten or more minutes of sheer madness as they all sniffed each other and found their pecking order. We left them to it once we realized there was going to be no doggy violence.

"Ah" said my mother. "Perfect timing. Dinner's nearly ready".

To me she said,

"You should go next door and meet Peter."

I was reluctant to leave Doc.

I was equally as reluctant to meet Peter.

My mother had cornered Doc, though, so I had to do this alone.

"Don't be long. You have fifteen minutes" she said.

So this was how I found myself knocking at the door of the Van Nord house.

The light shone through the frosted glass of the front door.

There was a giant shadow blocking the light, and the door was opened.

It was Peter.

His was the photo I'd grown so used to seeing in the frame on Mrs Van Nord's piano.

He wasn't just handsome.

He was movie star handsome, but not in a pretty boy kind of way.

He was rugged like some of the old time movie stars.

He was also incredibly tall, probably six foot six.

He had the physique of a hockey player.

"Hello?" he said.

His voice was like sand in chocolate.

"Hi" I said. "Peter? I'm Charlie. I was teaching your mother's students."

"Hi Charlie, come on in".

He guided me down the hall and into the living room where the upright piano stood, and his photo.

"What can I do for you?"

"Well first off, I'm so sorry about your mother. She was a fantastic woman" I told him.

"Thanks" he said.

I realized, from his silence, that I'd have to be the one to bring up the piano.

"Well, I guess you're wondering why I'm here".

He nodded.

I thought that, for an actor, he had few words.

"When Mrs Van Nord died my mother told me that YOUR mother had left me the piano in her will."

Peter looked at me with a sudden and furious thunder in his eyes.

He was certainly an intimidating figure and I felt very threatened by him, menace sparked off him like electricity.

"Look" he said. "I'm gonna be nice about this."
It didn't feel like he was going to be 'nice'.
"When my mother died she made no arrangements in her will for anyone except ME. I'm sorry pal. I don't know where you get your information, but it seems you're trying to trick me out of what's mine. The piano, this house, everything in it; it's all mine. Now I'm gonna ask you nicely to leave my property".
He herded me out of his house without another word and closed the door behind me.

I was back at my parents' house now.
"How did it go dear?" my mother asked.
"Apparently Mrs Van Nord DIDN'T leave me the piano in her will after all" I told her.
"Oh dear" she said. "Maybe she changed her mind".
"Yes, maybe that was it" I said.
"So tell me" she continued without pause "Is he as handsome as Mrs Van Nord said?"
"Incredibly handsome" I told her. "I think you'd like him".
She seemed to turn into a kitten before my eyes.
"Perhaps I'll take him over something to eat. It must be very traumatic for the poor boy, sorting through his dear mother's things. I'll keep a portion aside for him and take it over once we've eaten."
Riff raised an eyebrow ever so slightly.
"Good idea Dianne" he said. "I can spend some time with the boys here".
He waved his bottle of scotch at us, slightly, as he poured himself a drink.
I could never fault my mother for her cooking.

We ate well that night, although the conversation was a bit stilted and one-directional. The one direction it pointed to was always my mother.

By now Doc had realized, as had I, as had Riff, that my mother was at her best when she was being flattered. When the flattery stopped she found an excuse for a drama, and then she would take no prisoners.

Doc didn't really know this yet, but I certainly did.

Riff knew this too, I am sure.

"This is absolutely delicious Dianne, Charlie never mentioned you were such a great chef" said Doc.

"I'm sure he would never mention it. I'm only his mother. The one who fed him every day of his life" she said.

"Yes my darling" added Riff. "You managed to excel yourself. I don't know how you do it."

"Well it isn't easy; looking after everyone all the time. But that's what a mother does. And no one listens when you complain anyway, so I try my best; it's all anyone can do".

"And you do very well Dianne" Riff told her, but she didn't seem very appreciative of his comment. It was as if she had seen it as false flattery.

She didn't like that.

If this game was going to work then the rule first rule was that she must never see it is flattery.

Not fake flattery anyway.

"I hope it's all right" she said. "I find that lamb is such a delicate dish to prepare. Some people like it pink and other people can only stomach it if it's well done."

"Pink is good for me" said Doc.

"Me too" I added.

"I hope Peter, next door, likes it pink" she said.

"I'm certain he loves it pink" I said.

I couldn't resist knocking knees with Doc under the table.

I thought Riff was grinning ever so slightly too.
The dogs had all settled on various chairs around the open plan living room.
Scout was on the 'love seat', (as my mother called it), with Annabel.
I was happy enough that Scout would be well looked after while we were away in Ireland.
On that score alone it was a successful evening.
It was still early though.
I wanted to leave as soon as possible to avoid any possibility of catastrophe.
The longer we stayed the greater the chance of some sort of a melt-down.
It wasn't long before we had eaten our fill and every plate was empty.
Riff offered to clear the table so that my mother could more quickly deliver some food to Peter next door.
"Well, if you're sure darling" my mother said sweetly, (not in her absolute best china voice, but close enough).
"I'm sure darling" said Riff, and he kissed her on the cheek.
She made up a plate of food, which looked delicious, and vanished into the night.

Riff insisted that we all partake of his single malt.
I, for one, had no problem accepting.
Doc wondered which of us would be driving home, and if it was going to be him then he'd rather abstain.
"I have an idea" said Riff. "You can both stay the night".
Doc looked at me for some guidance.
I really didn't care about anything anymore.

I figured it wouldn't be long before bedtime anyway. Then, in the morning, we could be gone, (before too much trouble could be made).

"Go on then" said Doc, and Riff poured him a large measure.

As he poured Doc his drink he said,

"I know you two are lovers, and I'm happy for you. But we have to be careful in front of Dianne".

"I understand" said Doc, taking a sip.

"No, Des" Riff explained. "I don't think you DO understand. Dianne is of the old school. She would have every faggot, nigger, and Jew hanged if she could. That's not my feeling, I want to tell you that. But it's HERS. God knows I've tried. But nothing will ever change that".

"Okay" Doc said. "I get it".

"If you want to stay the night then you're both welcome. If you're lucky you might get to share a bed tonight, but I'm not making any promises".

I think now, looking back, that Riff was only looking for a bit of male company. Or any company other than my mother's.

Maybe he was thinking that misery needs company!

The reality was, (or one of the realities was), that Doc and I were too drunk to drive, and we had Scout with us, so there was no need to hurry anywhere.

In a sane world there would be no reason to go anywhere. This wasn't a sane world.

I think we WANTED to believe that we were living in a sane world.

I also believe that a good meal, followed by good scotch, can sway a man to go against what he knows is right.

One of the things that made me think we should stay was the fact that I would be playing in church the next day.

It seemed a waste of time and energy to drive back into town, then drive back here tomorrow.

It was one of those occasions when logic won out over emotion.

Emotion SCREAMED that we should go home.

Logic calmly dictated that it was best if we stayed.

The dogs rushed to the front door as my mother let herself in.

She was carrying an empty plate, which had not long ago been full of lamb and roast potatoes.

"Peter's a hungry boy then" quipped Riff.

"Not anymore" said my mother.

She looked as proud as she could be.

"Isn't he handsome?" she asked.

Since I was the only one who knew what he looked like I felt impelled to answer.

"He looks like a movie star".

"Oh he's even more handsome than that" she said, though I'm not sure how that was possible, but she soon explained.

"He's like a god, so tall and rugged".

Riff poured us all another drink.

"I should have asked him if he has a girlfriend" she said.

"I'm surprised you didn't" said Riff.

"We're not ALL obsessed with sex darling" she hissed.

"Aren't we?" he countered.

I knew who was going to win this skirmish.

Riff should have known too.

"No we're not!" she took the plate into the kitchen. "Peter is the perfect gentleman".

"Did he say anything about the piano?" I wanted to know.

"Forget about the piano dear. I apologised for you and all is forgiven, so don't worry about it any more".

"Apologised for me?" I frowned.

"Yes dear. Peter thought it was a bit crass to come round the minute that his mother was dead, but I smoothed it all out. That's what a mother does."

Riff changed the subject.

"Charlie and the professor have decided to stay the night".

"Oh, that's lovely, I should make up a bed" she said, and began bustling about looking for fresh bed linen.

I had an idea that Riff's trick, with my mother, was to keep her busy. That way she had less time to attack him.

It seemed to be working well for him.

Doc couldn't resist saying "You DO know I'm not a professor, don't you Riff?"

"Sure, but if I called you anything else Madam wouldn't understand who the fuck I was talking about!"

Dennis chuckled.

Thankfully my mother was already out of earshot, or she would have pounced on Riff from a great height for calling her 'madam' and using the 'F' word.

"I hope you two won't mind sharing a double bed" she said on her return. "I assumed that, being good friends, it wouldn't be too much of a problem, but if it is then I can make up another bed".

"I'm pretty certain the boys can keep their hands to themselves" Riff grinned.

"Riff, can you please refrain from being quite so disgusting!" my mother huffed angrily.

"It's just that, you know, I'm at sea half the year, on a submarine" he winked at Doc. "I know what some of the lads get up to!"

"Well THESE boys are not ON your submarine Riff, and you can leave all that dirty talk behind you thank you very much!" my mother fumed.

"Gee, Dianne, I was just having fun" he said.

"We don't want that kind of fun here!" she answered.
"I don't know about Charlie but I'd be happy enough to sleep anywhere" interjected Doc.
"Me too mum. Thanks for making up a bed" I added.
"You're both very welcome" she said, very pleased with herself that she'd kept the Devil at bay.
"I would love to know how the two of you met" said Doc.
"Riff was stationed in England. I had just divorced Charlie's father. I was involved socially with the navy back then, organizing various charity events and so on. Riff attended some 'do' or other that I'd organized. Our eyes met across a crowded room and we fell in love, didn't we darling?" she said, as if it was a prepared speech.
"That's exactly how it happened" he said. "And, boy, if I could do it all again..." he paused for effect. My mother frowned. "I'd do it in an instant!" He finished.
"Yes well" said my mother. "I can't say that I would!"
"You seem like the ideal couple" Doc told them both.
"Yes, everyone says that" said my mother, and she smiled sweetly at Riff rather suddenly. "Don't they darling".
"Yes Dianne. They surely do".
It seemed to me like we were watching a romantic play with two very bad actors playing the lead roles.
I felt a bit sick.
I looked at my watch.
It wasn't THAT late, but it was late enough.
I could play my church organ trump card.
"I feel so tired" I said. "And I have to play the organ tomorrow. Will anyone mind if I go to bed?"
"I feel a bit tired too" said Doc. "Will you think it rude if we cut the night short?"
"Not at all. You boys get some sleep" said Riff.

"Well I was hoping to spend a bit of time with my son and the professor, but I suppose it's okay. The bed is made up" said my mother.

She was mightily put out, but she accepted it with as much good grace as she could muster.

"Tomorrow is another day" said Riff.

We said our goodnights and went to bed.

Scout saw what was happening.

He followed us into our bedroom.

Scout slept on our bed, with us, as he did every night.

Doc and I had no intention of making love that night.

I had a dream that night.

I was in the Van Nord house.

Peter was at the piano.

He was singing to me in his sand and chocolate voice.

"Hush little baby don't you cry
Daddy's gonna sing you a lullaby
A lullaby like you never heard
Daddy's gonna buy you a mockin' bird
If that mockin' bird don't sing
Daddy's gonna buy you a diamond ring
If that diamond ring don't shine
Daddy's gonna be your Valentine"

When Peter finished singing there was a knock at the door.

It was my mother bringing him a plate of lamb.

Before my mother could come into the room Peter lifted the top of the piano, folded me in two, and bundled me into the piano.

My mother then came in and gave Peter the lamb.

Peter scraped all the lamb into the piano and handed my mother back the empty plate.

I woke up from the dream.
I was cuddled into Doc as close as a person could be.
I felt safe.

Then I became fully conscious and knew I was in my mother's house.
Suddenly I didn't feel so safe.
I got up, washed myself in the bathroom, dressed, made coffee, and prepared to play church organ.
Doc didn't wake up so easily so I left him there in bed, sleeping.
Instead I took Scout for a walk.

Scout wanted to cross the road into the wood. The same wood where Duffy had crawled to.
I let Scout lead.
Sure enough Scout soon had us at the same tree where I had found Duffy.
Scout sniffed around, wagging his tail.
There was something half hidden in the dirt and leaves.
There was a glint of light.
I hunkered down for a closer look.
I brushed away dirt and leaves.
There was a blade.
I found the handle and pulled a small dagger from the earth.
The dagger was filthy, as you'd expect, so I spent a few minutes cleaning the handle and blade.
The handle looked like it was made from bone of some kind.
The blade didn't look modern, not that I was an expert.
The dagger was only about six inches long.

The handle had strange carvings along both sides, and looked to me like they were carved by hand a long time ago.

The carving was intricate but I couldn't be sure what it represented.

I put it away in my pocket and persuaded Scout that his walk was over now.

We went back to my mother's house.

Riff was awake, making coffee.

"I'm making pancakes, want some?" he asked.

"Oh yes, please"

I poured myself a fresh coffee.

I don't know what possessed me to ask, but once it was out of my mouth it was too late anyway.

"Are you happy Riff?"

He didn't answer immediately.

"Happy enough I guess" he said, after much thought.

"Is that what happens?" I wanted to know. "A life of hard work, and struggle, and doing what's right. And you're happy enough?"

"A bit deep for a Sunday morning isn't it Charlie?"

"I just found a knife, in the woods across the road. Exactly where I found Duffy that night".

"Let me see" he said, filled with curiosity.

I showed him.

"Isn't that something?" he said, turning it over and over in his hand.

He handed it back to me.

"Well? What do you think?" I asked him.

"It's a cool little knife. What are you gonna do with it?"

"I don't know. I thought it might MEAN something; finding it in the same place I found Duffy that night".

"It's just a knife Charlie. That's all".

The stack of pancakes was building now.
"Don't think about it too much Charlie. Have some pancakes."

Doc was up and joined us for pancakes.
Then my mother was up too.
I didn't want to be around my mother for too long, not right now.
I told Doc I'd need to get to the church.
So we left Scout at my mother's and headed church-wards.

Riff and my mother didn't know that Doc and I were going on holiday together.
They still thought Scout was staying with them because of the house move.

"I hope you don't mind" Doc said as we drove to the church. "When you went next door to talk to your neighbour about the piano I was talking to your mother."
This sounded ominous.
"No, it was fine," he said. "She showed me a picture of Jim Watson!"
"Why on earth would she do that?" I asked.
"I hope you don't mind" he explained. "I asked her".
I didn't understand.
"I wanted to know what he looked like".
"Why would you want to know what he looked like?" I asked him.
"I hoped it would give me an insight into what you were going through. Anyway, she let me keep the picture".
"I didn't know she kept any pictures" I said.
"There was another reason I wanted to have a photo of him" he explained. "I thought that it might help, if one day you decided you wanted to trace him".

"What? I don't want to trace him!"
"Not now, but one day you might", he said.
"And does my mother think that we're going to try to trace my father?"
"No, she just thinks I was being sentimental".
"Well, that's okay, I guess".

I found myself experiencing an ever growing feeling of dread.
I'm trying to pinpoint the exact moment it started.
I thought it started the moment I found the knife but in fact it had started a little while before.
During that Sunday I began to feel slightly sick, as if I'd eaten something bad.
At first that's all I thought it was.
I figured that the next day I'd probably feel better.
The next day was ever so slightly worse.
I knew I wasn't suffering from food poisoning.
I knew exactly what the feeling was; a feeling of dread.
The question was; what was I dreading?
Maybe I was dreading the move into our new house.
We needed professional movers because of the grand piano.
A window had to be taken out, and a crane hired.
The double bed went the same way, just because it was easier.
Everything else was taken down in the lift.
By the evening we had all of our belongings in the new house.
It didn't take too long to get everything sorted out.
Everything we owned had been in a one bedroom apartment.

Now we could spread everything over two floors, four bedrooms, two reception rooms, and even a guest-house. The house still looked empty.

There was the grand piano and a few other substantial pieces of furniture, but we realized we might need to look around for more stuff.

Anyway, we had moved in, and the feeling of dread was still there.

It was eating away at the pit of my stomach like a worm.

We'd invited a few people over to our house warming.

Perhaps this feeling if dread somehow had something to do with the house warming.

Roger had helped us with the move and then decided to stay, since he was going to be our lodger anyway.

We didn't have a bed he could sleep on, so until we bought one for him he had to sleep on the couch.

The dagger that I'd found, with the strange markings, I put in a drawer, but for some reason I never showed Doc.

We had the phone connected, using the same phone number from the apartment.

For a short time it was very much like camping out, and it would have been fun except for this terrible feeling of dread.

I told Doc and he suggested I see the doctor and get some pills for it.

I was reluctant but I went anyway.

I was prescribed some Valium.

I wondered around in a bit of a daze for a while, but the feeling of dread didn't go away.

I had a supply of the tablets, taking at least one a day.

It was the day of the house warming.

There was plenty of food and drink.
Rob and Al were there, of course.
It wouldn't have been a party without them.
Mick and Ursie Passion Flower had left for Europe.
Barb and Mark came though.
They brought a gift with them.
It was a big marijuana plant, from Mick.
It was a house warming gift and thank-you present.
Von Chanel was there and brought his guitar.
The party came and went.
It was a great evening although nothing memorable happened.
Rob and Al didn't pull any of their tricks.
I thought that was a shame.

The next morning there was still a huge feeling of dread.
We'd be travelling to Ireland in a day or two.
Scout was with my parents.
Everything had been arranged.
I still felt as if I'd forgotten something.
My thoughts were confused.
I had to look at the time-table I kept.
I had no more piano lessons to teach, not until September.
Bette had organized a stand-in organist while I was away.
I had already quit work at the Fisherman's.
I'd booked holiday leave with Harold's house.
The term at university had finished and would start again in September.
On paper, at least, it looked like everything had been neatly planned and executed.
Then why did it feel as if I'd forgotten something crucial?
Maybe I really HAD forgotten something.
In spite of Valium I couldn't shake off the terrible feeling.

It festered in my gut like a poisonous tapeworm.
The worm roiled without rest.
The feeling of dread got deeper and became all pervasive.

Chapter Five

I had flown before and hated it.
Every flight was like a living nightmare for me.
I would grab the arms of the seat and hold on so tight that
my knuckles went white.
I had never been able to partake of the in-flight meal or
drinks.
I knew this time would be no different.
I wondered if my feeling of dread was some psychic
message that we were going to die in a plane crash.
I decided to take some Valium for the flight.
It made me very groggy but that was okay.
We were landing in Dublin airport before we knew it.

We hired a car and were soon on our way to Mary and
Agnes, (Doc's aunt and cousin).
We drove North, along the East coast of Ireland, with the
Irish Sea almost always in sight. Mary and Agnes lived in
a little fishing village on this route.
I felt jet-lagged, as did Doc, I know.
I felt drowsy from the Valium.
More than that though I still couldn't shake off this dread
in my stomach.
"You're looking a bit pale there soldier" said Doc.

I told him that I still had the bad feeling, and there was pain in his face.

"You think it's a premonition?" he asked.

I said I didn't know, maybe it was.

It was a beautiful Summer day, only a few white clouds in the sky coming in from the East.

We'd been driving for about two hours.

We were about to drive into a small, and typical, Irish village.

I could see a pub, and a Post Office.

There was a butcher's, a hardware store, and various other little shops on either side of the street.

There was a young woman on a bicycle, wearing a long pink dress with short sleeves, and a big straw hat.

She was very pretty, with long dark hair.

There was a basket on the front of her bike, and in the basket were a loaf and other groceries.

"That looks like Agnes" exclaimed Doc, slowing the car to a stop.

He opened the window and shouted "Agnes! Over here!" and waved.

"Hello cousin" she said sweetly and calmly, as if seeing her cousin was an everyday occurrence.

"Good to see you" he said, getting out of the car to give her a big hug.

She was holding on to her bike with one hand, and this made the hug a little awkward.

I noticed she had a bandage on one of her arms.

It was in the same place where I would normally have cut myself.

I wondered if she cut herself too.

"This is my travel companion, Charlie" Doc said to her.

"And this is my cousin Agnes" he said to me.

I got out of the car to shake her hand, (she'd let go of Doc by now).

"Hello Charlie" she said.

"Very nice to meet you, Agnes" I said.

There was something otherworldly about Agnes.

She could have passed for an Elfin Queen, I thought.

I noticed an ornament around her neck.

It was a string of dark beads with a long pendant made of carved bone.

The markings on the bone looked strangely familiar.

I realized, with sudden horror, that they reminded me of the dagger I'd found in the wood so recently.

I didn't have the dagger with me. It was in a drawer in the bedroom of our new house.

I had nothing to compare, only my memory.

Even so, I thought the markings had to be the same.

Agnes caught me looking at her pendant.

"Pretty, isn't it?" she said, fingering it. Her tone was whimsical and like a distant folk-song.

"It's unusual" I said.

This obviously wasn't the answer she wanted because she dismissed me.

She turned her attention to Doc instead.

"I have wee bit of shopping to do. Why don't you head up to the house? Mummy's opened up the guest house for you. I'll meet up with you in an hour or so" and she mounted her bike with a smile and cycled off.

"She never seems to age" said Doc.

"When did you see her last?" I wanted to know.

"Let me think. I guess it was about fifteen years ago. She looks exactly the same".

"How old would she have been, fifteen years ago?"

"I guess she was about thirty".
"No, I don't believe it! You're telling me she's forty five?"
I said in amazement.
"Oh yes. She's older than me by about six years."
That seemed incredible.
"There must be something in the water" I said.

We drove on and found the turning.
There was a sign that read Ivy Lodge.
Ivy Lodge was situated up a long drive.
It was a small Georgian building, perfectly symmetrical.
There were pillars at each side of the front door and ivy
growing over the façade of the building.
"If I remember right then the guest house Agnes
mentioned is about a quarter mile behind the main house".
"I wasn't expecting this" I said. "It's all very grand. I
imagined it would be a cottage or something."
"Ah" he said. "The Irish archetype! No, they have
plumbing, electricity, television, telephones, everything
that we have."
"Well, that's me well and truly told off" I said.
Doc chuckled.
A slim blonde woman came out of the house to meet us.
She was smiling warmly at Doc.
"Hello there" she said.
Doc hugged her tightly for a good minute or two.
"So good to see you Auntie Mary. I missed you so much"
he said.
The love between aunt and nephew was so obvious that I
could feel it radiate off them like heat.
"And who's this handsome fella?" she said, finally letting
go.
"This is Charlie."

"Well hello there Charlie. I want you to make yourself right at home."

She hugged me too and then guided us into the house. "We can sort your luggage later. You'll be in the guest house, though I have to warn you there are some other guests about to arrive, either tonight or tomorrow, depending on the roads".

"Oh?" exclaimed Doc.

"It was a last minute phone call. A small group of lads are coming up from Limerick to do some business. I'm sure they'll be no bother, so they won't."

It transpired that Mary made her living by renting out rooms in her guest house.

We were in her large kitchen.

There was a peat fired range, with a steaming kettle. Mary made us a pot of tea.

"I imagine you'll be tired after your trip. I'll make you a bite to eat and then you can both get a bath. That may wake you both up a bit and we can have a wee hoolie if you like. Or you can sleep for a few hours to get over your jet-lag."

The large kitchen window had a mountain view, clouds were gathering at the peaks of the mountains.

"You made it just in time" said Mary. ""There'll be a storm tonight, so there will".

"Now" said Mary, sitting down at last. "Tell me all your news."

Doc then told Mary about his separation, the new house, the new dog.

Mary made all the right encouraging noises.

"Oh dear" she said, when Doc told her about Sandra and the break up.

"These things happen. I'm sure you did your best".

When Doc finished with his news Mary said, "I'm sure you'll want to see your mam's grave while your here. It's her anniversary on Sunday and there'll be a mass".

Doc knew this, he said, (although he hadn't made me aware of it).

Of course Doc had a history. I had been so caught up in my own history that I had never even thought to ask about HIS! It was further proof that I was going through life wearing a blindfold. I hated myself for this negative quality and swore I would change it.

When Doc had told his story Mary turned her attention to me.

"And how do you know my favourite nephew here?" she asked me.

Doc took over.

I guess he wanted us to keep our story straight, and the story was NOT going to include the fact that we were lovers.

"Well it's nice that Desmond has a good friend, so it is. Good friends are so hard to find."

The old house was making a new sound now. There was the opening and closing of the big front door, footsteps, and the kitchen door opened.

It was Agnes.

"Hello" she said, in that same faery voice. She carried her shopping to the big wooden table, dumped it all there as if it meant nothing to her.

Mary was about to introduce me to Agnes, but was cut short.

"Oh, we all met up in the village just now" said Agnes.

"Lovely" said Mary. "Then you can get yourselves settled in at the guest house. You can have a bath, even a wee sleep if you like. Supper will be ready at about eight. How's that?"

"What's for supper?" asked Doc.

"Well my darling" said Mary. "It's a special occasion. I never see my nephew, so we'll be having steaks."

"Fresh from the butcher" added Agnes, and she pointed to the table.

On the table, among all the other shopping, was a bag full of red meat.

I knew that I wasn't hungry right at this minute. I was more interested in a bath and a nap. I knew that I certainly WOULD be ready for a steak just as soon as I was refreshed from the journey.

I was able to look at Mary and Agnes, mother and daughter, and compare them.

It didn't seem feasible that Agnes could have even reached her thirties, (but according to Doc she was forty five).

I looked at Mary with her youthful figure and posture.

I thought she couldn't be older than forty, but she would have to be in her sixties.

I had to mention this.

"I hope you don't think I'm being rude. I can't see how the two of you can look so young" I said.

"Ah" said Mary. "That'll be the good clean air and water. And all the virtuous living" she laughed.

I looked at Dennis, comparing him to his relatives.

I could see a resemblance, around the jawline and the eyes.

His cheekbones were high, like theirs.

I could see they were all of the same family.

More than this I realized that Dennis had also retained a youthful look.

He was almost forty now, yet he could pass for thirty.
Younger, if he changed his glasses and got a decent
haircut.
I know that I looked young too, but then I WAS young. I
was still not yet twenty one.

There was a narrow dirt track that ran between the main
house and the guest house. Doc and I drove down the track
and the storm began to break, as Mary had foretold.
It was about four in the afternoon, but storm clouds made
it seem later in the day.
In another four hours we could have a steak supper, but in
the meantime we could bathe and nap.

Once we were alone in the guest house I hugged Doc close
to me.
It felt like an age since we'd had any physical closeness.
I missed it.
I needed it, especially now.
There were three bedrooms in the guest house, which was
much more like the cottage I'd imagined.
The bedrooms each contained two single beds.
Mary had stuck a note to one of the bedroom doors.
'Desmond and friend. This is your room'.
We dumped all our luggage in our bedroom.
We both had a bath.
Then we went to bed.
We shared a single bed, holding each other close.
I guess it was about seven.
Thunder and lightning made it difficult to fall asleep.
It seemed the perfect time to make love.

Since the night of our foursome our love-making had become more adventurous, but on this night it was simple and gentle.

He held my head in his two hands and kissed my forehead, eyes and cheeks.

I explored his manly body with my fingers, paying attention to his nipples, tweaking and pulling them.

Then we were kissing each other passionately.

Neither of us needed to climax.

This time it wasn't about that so much as recapturing something we'd lost.

Even so, we climaxed together.

Breathless and sweating we lay there and listened to the storm.

"Better mess up the other bed, in case anyone puts two and two together. You never know". Doc was thinking like a character in an Agatha Christie novel.

We rolled onto the other bed together, and before we knew it we were making love again.

If anything the second time was better than the first.

The storm still raged but I felt calm and at peace.

It was fast approaching eight o'clock.

We dressed and then we drove our hire car down the dirt track to the main house.

"That's good" said Mary. "You look rested now, so you do".

We were all in the kitchen and mother and daughter were bustling about with their separate duties.

"Agnes, did you start the fire in the dining room?" asked Mary.

"Yes" she answered, but I thought I heard just a hint of resentment in her voice.

"And is the table set?"

"Yes it IS mother!" and there it was, that resentment, less veiled now.

"And candles?"

"All lit. Everything's done mother".

"Then show our guests to the dining room Agnes, and I can serve".

Agnes showed us into the dining room, which was a grand affair, with marble fireplace and chandelier.

The table had been laid with white linen table cloth, matching napkins, shining cutlery and crystal.

Doc and I had the forethought to buy wine from the airport duty free, which was our gift to the table tonight.

Doc and I found our places at the table. Then he got up again, saying we needed a corkscrew.

I was left with Agnes as she finished setting the table by placing steak knives by every napkin.

I could hear Doc and Mary sharing laughter and conversation in the kitchen.

I figured our meal would be served in five minutes or so but I was comfortable with the wait.

I could smell lavender, and I suddenly thought of Mrs Van Nord.

I suppose my eyes must have watered slightly because Agnes was suddenly saying something to me.

"You think you're special, don't you?" she asked.

"We're all special, in my opinion" I answered.

"Well YOU'RE not that special, I can tell".

I noticed that she had replaced the bandage on her forearm with a fresh one.

"I'm quite happy NOT to be special" I told her.

"I speak to the dead" she informed me "and they tell me things!"

The feeling of dread, almost forgotten, was beginning to rise up from the pit of my stomach.

I didn't know what was going on.

"They told me about YOU".

I was intrigued, in spite of the dread.

"And what do these dead people say?" I asked.

"Don't you mock me!" her voice was rising in volume and pitch.

Her eyes were wild.

I was reminded of the Keats poem.

'I closed her wild wild eyes with kisses four.

"Don't you EVER mock me" she hissed at me.

"I'm sorry Agnes. I didn't mean anything!"

She had one last steak knife to place, at MY setting.

She held onto the knife, caressing the handle.

"They warned me about you" she hissed again. "They said to beware!"

"I'm not a threat to you Agnes."

I could still hear laughter from the kitchen.

'Please hurry back' I was thinking.

"But you ARE a threat" she said. "Nothing I can't handle though" and she laughed quietly to herself.

"I think you and I must have got off on the wrong foot somehow Agnes. Can we start again?" I said, trying to calm her.

"NO!" she screamed, and then she lunged at me with the knife.

She brought the knife straight down onto the table.

My left hand was in the way.

The blade broke right through the skin between my thumb and forefinger and stuck in the table.

I screamed with pain and shock.

Blood poured out onto the white linen.

Agnes screamed, louder than I had.

She ran from the room, screaming "He stabbed himself. He just stabbed himself!"

My right hand was on the handle of the knife now.

I tried the best I could to push my left hand back down on the table, and with my right I pulled the knife out of the wood beneath, and then back out through through the broken flesh.

Dennis and Mary entered the dining room, with Agnes right behind.

"SEE!" Agnes screamed. "He stabbed himself. Right in front of my eyes. I never saw such a thing!"

I suppose it must have looked as if I had indeed just stabbed myself.

I was holding the knife!

Doc came over to me and looked at my bloody left hand.

"What happened?" he asked me gently.

I looked at Agnes, and it seemed she was daring me to tell what happened.

'Tell the truth and you'll regret it' I imagined her thinking.

Mary rushed from the room and came back a little later with bandages, cotton wool and sticky plaster.

Doc had my hand wrapped in a napkin now.

"You brought a madman into our house Desmond. Why would you do that?" screamed Agnes hysterically.

"I'll call the doctor" said Mary.

"It's okay. I won't need a doctor" I told her.

"Not for you" Mary clarified. "For Agnes".

I didn't know what this meant.

Doc cleaned up the blood and then bandaged me.

For some reason I was feeling guilty about the blood on the lovely white linen.

"Sorry about all this" I said.

"That's okay" Doc said. "Tell me what happened."
We were alone in the dining room now.
"It was Agnes" I explained.
I was aware that what I was about to say would seem unbelievable.
"She got herself all angry over something, saying she could speak to the dead, and that they'd warned her about me. Then she just lunged at me suddenly".
Mary had taken Agnes through to the kitchen.
I could hear Mary trying to calm Agnes, but Agnes was screaming,
"Get him out of our house!"
Doc kissed me on the forehead.
"Let me get you out of here" he said.

The storm was still raging as Doc drove me back to the guest house.
"Maybe this is what your premonition was all about" he suggested.
"Maybe" I said, as he put me into bed and tucked me in.
"I really don't want to leave you but I have to go back to the house" he said.
I didn't want him to go.
"I'll wait there for the doctor, and then bring him up here so he can have a look at you".
I told him I was fine. I didn't need to be looked at.
He produced a bottle of scotch, and then found a glass.
"You'll need this" he said. "You've suffered a shock".
I took a sip, with my good hand.
It was shaking.
"I'll be back as quick as I can" he said.
He was about to leave but turned around at the door.

"Mary's expecting some guys from Limerick. They might be here tonight. They shouldn't bother you".
"I'm sure I can look after myself. I'll be okay".
He left then.

I tried to figure out what happened with Agnes.
I went through the events of the day in my mind.
Everything seemed somehow to hinge on me recognizing the pendant that Agnes wore around her neck.
I was more confused now, but tried to drown it all with more scotch.
I took a Valium.
Agnes was obviously dangerous.
I'd guessed already, right from our first meeting, that she was most likely a self-harmer, as I had once been.
Something I had done must have triggered off her dangerous behaviour, but I couldn't just put it all down to my comment about her pendant.
I was missing something.
I had to take my blindfold off.
I tried to think harder, but the scotch wasn't helping.
Nevertheless I poured myself another glass.
I hoped it might send me to sleep.
There was still thunder and lightning, and sleep proved impossible.

Doc was beside me.
The bedside light was on.
I felt a sharp pain and was reminded of my wound, and then the events of the day spilled back into my mind.
"The doctor's here to have a look at you" he said in his gentlest voice.

Behind Doc, in the shadow, was a thin man wearing round spectacles.

"Hello Charlie, I just want to make sure you're okay" he said.

He felt my pulse, and shone a light into my eyes.

He looked at my hand.

He undid the bandage, congratulated Doc on his nursing skills, then bandaged me up again with a fresh dressing.

"Now, if this young lady attacked you, as you say, then you really MUST inform the police. She's sedated now, so you're quite safe for the moment, if what you say is true."

I didn't want to be in this position.

I didn't want to have to justify myself.

I was innocent.

I felt no one would believe me.

I decided that the best course of action was to do nothing.

"No, I don't want to call the police" I said.

The doctor grunted, sounding displeased.

"If you aren't prepared to call the police then this will look like you harmed yourself. Are you sure you want that?" he asked me.

"No police" I reiterated.

"It's your choice. I'll give you some tablets. They'll help you deal with the shock" he said.

He left a small container on the bedside table, looked at me one last time, then left the room.

I could hear other voices in the guest house.

They sounded masculine and boisterous.

"Who else is here?" I asked Doc.

"Mary's guests from Limerick arrived a little while ago, in a white van. They shouldn't bother you. Take one of those tablets and try to get to sleep. I'm going to spend the night

in the main house. We have a drama with Agnes. Well,
you of all people would know that!"
He kissed me on the lips, ruffled my hair.
He picked up a little bag which I guessed contained his
toiletries.
"I'll see you in the morning" he said, and then he was
gone.
I could hear Doc's voice talking to someone in the hall
outside my room.
I couldn't hear the words. It was a mumble from where I
was situated.
Maybe he was talking to the Limerick men.
Then he was gone.

Once Doc had gone I still found it very hard to get to
sleep.
In spite of the Valium and the scotch I was wide awake.
The storm had died down now, but in its place was the
masculine, boisterous noise of the Limerick men.
Someone was running a bath.
I needed to use the toilet desperately.
I knew it was a shared bathroom.
There was only one bathroom in the guest house.
I held on for as long as I could but the sound of running
bath water only made things worse.
I threw on a T-shirt and a pair of boxer shorts.
I crept out of the bedroom as quietly as I could and made it
to the bathroom.
The bathroom door was open and at the sink was a broad
bald man, wearing just a towel, shaving foam around his
goatee beard and on his bald scalp.
I was stunned.
It looked like Jim Watson, my father.

Surely this was a dream.

How could my father have found me here?

The bald man turned round to me, aware of my presence through his peripheral vision.

"Yo" he said. "You must be Charlie. Mary, and yer man, told us you were here."

It was uncanny.

This man was the identical twin of my father, Jim.

The tattoos on his arms weren't identical, but that was a minor detail.

I noticed that, unlike my father, this man had numerous scars. Some looked like they might have been knife wounds and others might have been bullet wounds. None looked like the scars of a self harmer.

"Yes, I'm Charlie" I confessed.

"Good to meet you. I'm Jim" he said, and I was stunned at that.

Another Jim!

"Jim Fox, but everyone calls me Jim".

"You'll meet the boys in a bit" he said. "Do you need to have a tinkle?" he asked.

It was such a dainty word coming from such a big man.

"Yes, I'm busting" I admitted.

"Don't mind me, I've seen it all before" he said.

"Erm" I muttered shyly.

"Jeez boy, I'm not going to jump ya!" he barked.

I had a 'tinkle' as Jim had called it.

Jim carried on talking to me as he shaved.

"Me and the lads had a spot of business to do here, and now we can party" he explained. "Go and say hello to the lads when you're done here."

With that he turned off the taps, pulled off his towel, and hopped into the bathwater as if I wasn't there.

The bath was parallel to the toilet, and Jim had positioned himself so he could face me while he talked.

"So what's your story?" he asked. I felt his eyes drinking in my every detail.

I'd finished my 'tinkle' and said,

"Here on a holiday".

"With your boyfriend?" he chuckled. "Was that your boyfriend who just left there?"

I didn't know what to say.

"I'm just messing with ya" he said, laughing.

"Okay" I said.

"Give me ten minutes and I'll catch up with you, just as soon as I've finished wi' me bath."

I left the bathroom with an empty bladder and went straight back to my room.

I wasn't quite ready to meet a group of burly men intent on a party.

I poured myself a scotch.

After about ten minutes there was a knock on my door, together with Jim Fox's gravelly voice telling me to,

"Get out here and join the party Charlie".

I thought to myself 'what the hell', and pulled on a pair of jeans.

I opened the door, and there was Jim, dressed only in his boxers.

"Come and meet the lads. They're a boring bunch o' cunts, but what can ye do? Maybe ye can liven up the proceedings" he said.

The thought of me livening up proceedings was hopeful at best, but not likely.

I was fascinated by Jim's physical appearance.

His arms, legs and chest were as thick as my father's. His neck, too, was twenty inches round, at least.

Jim's belly was like an over-inflated football, with the skin stretched tight over years of beer and good food.

His chest, back, arms and legs had a thick covering of blond hair.

There was no doubt that Jim looked intimidating, but his manner was jovial.

"These are the lads; Anto meet Charlie, Charlie meet Anto, Brian meet Charlie, Charlie meet Brian".

We all nodded and grunted our hellos.

Anto and Brian didn't look at me directly, but I felt them weighing me up out of the corner of their eyes when I wasn't looking.

"We're gonna have a friendly game of poker. Will ye join us?" asked Jim Fox.

"I have no money" I said. Doc had been in charge of our cash.

"Don't ye be worryin' about that! We're using chips" he explained.

So that's how I came to be playing poker with three strange men.

Jim, I have to add, was the only one in his boxers.

Everyone else wore jeans and T-shirt.

"Get rid of that will ye? Ye fuckin' eejit" Jim said to Brian.

Brian was quick to pick something up from the table before I could see it.

"Burn it, ya prick".

Brian set fire to it.

I couldn't tell if it was a receipt or a ticket of some kind. Perhaps it was a photo.

Brian lit a cigarette from the flames and blew out a cloud of smoke.

I'd never played poker before.
They taught me the rules in minutes.
Jim produced a bottle of Southern Comfort and poured everyone a hefty measure.
I was already a bit drunk but I promised myself that I'd pace the drinking after this.
These men were obviously seasoned drinkers.
I was more of a beer drinker, or occasionally a wine drinker.
Spirits were something I usually avoided, mostly because of the hangover the next day.
Tonight, though, I didn't care so much.
I'd been through so much today already. I didn't think anything else could go wrong.
I was going to enjoy myself for a change.
Jim won the first hand.
"You are a big fat cunt Jimbo. I'm sure ya marked the cards" said Anto.
Anto was large-framed, like a farmer, with a big moon face.
I guessed he was about thirty, and was surprised to hear he was only three years older than me.
"Don't ye be calling me a cunt Anto, I'm warning you!" said Jim.
Anto grunted.
Another hand was dealt out.
I ended up winning that hand, with a full house.
"That's the way to do it" said Jim, patting me on the back.
Though Jim was smiling, laughing, grinning and joking all the time I still felt he held hidden menace.
I put that feeling aside, and put it all down to the fact that he resembled my father so closely.

There was no reason to paint Jim Fox with the same brush I usually painted Jim Watson.

"So tell us all Charlie. Are you one of these faggot boys and that's your boyfriend down in the big house there?" asked Jim.

I shook my head, refusing to be drawn out.

"We're all friends here now Charlie. You tell us now, and we'll all tell you something" he said.

"Oh, I don't know about that" I said.

"The way I see it is this" said Jim. "He's your daddy, would that be what he is?" Jim was insistent.

"We're just friends" I said.

"Well I don't believe that, not for a second" he mocked.

Anto and Brian were obviously greatly amused at my discomfort.

I got the feeling that Jim might be in the habit of humiliating and bullying his two comrades.

I was probably just a bit of light relief.

Jim put his arm round my shoulder and said conspiratorially,

"I'll tell you Charlie, and maybe that will put you at your ease. Me and the lads here deal in a bit of coke".

Anto and Brian didn't look well pleased at Jim's confession, but he winked at them and they seemed to relax.

"We're the bad guys" he said. "The ones your mammy warned you about".

I laughed at that.

"Don't laugh at me Charlie, it's the truth. Let me show you."

He left the room and came back a minute later, carrying a sports bag.

He put the bag on the counter that separated the kitchen from the living area.

"Leave it be Jimbo" said Brian.

"Yeah, Jim, no one needs to know" added Anto.

"Shut up ya shower o' cunts" he said.

He left the sports bag where it was for the moment and returned to the poker table.

"Will your boyfriend be back here tonight?" asked Jim.

I wasn't exactly annoyed by these constant taunts, I was just uncomfortable, and maybe even bored by them.

I had an idea that Jim might even have tendencies himself, but I certainly wasn't going to be the one to suggest THAT!

I thought it very possible that Jim had done his fair share of experimenting.

"First he's not my boyfriend, and second he's free to come and go; so I don't know what he plans to do tonight."

I wanted Jim to think that there was a possibility that Doc MIGHT be back tonight, though I knew he wouldn't be.

"You sound like you were very well brought up Charlie, would that be right?" Jim asked me.

"I don't know about that" I said.

He poured us all another drink.

"I think it's time lads" said Jim suddenly. "Let's show Lord Fauntleroy how we party!"

He went to the sports bag and pulled out a smaller bag made of clear plastic.

It looked like it contained about half a pound of icing sugar.

I'd never seen coke before, let alone tried it, but I knew this WAS coke, and that is was probably the good stuff.

The one thing I guessed was that it was a much bigger amount than could be said was for personal use!

He spilled some of the white powder onto the counter-top and began to make it into lines using a credit card, also in the sports bag.

"Ah Jimbo, there's no need for that!" whined Anto.

"Shut yer hole" shouted Jim. "Who's in charge here?"

"You're the boss Jimbo" admitted Anto.

"That's better".

Jim had made about ten lines.

Then he rolled up a note and took a snort.

His eyes were suddenly wide.

"That's better" he laughed and handed Anto the note.

Anto did a line then passed the note to Brian.

Brian did a line and passed the note to me.

I refused at first, but all eyes were on me now.

I gave up any resistance and snorted a line.

Everything was suddenly very clear, as if I was seeing things with new eyes, hearing things with new ears.

"That's the spirit Charlie boy" said Jim.

I felt like I'd passed some rite into manhood. I'd been accepted by these strangers now.

"What happened to your hand?" asked Brian.

I couldn't begin to say what happened so I just said it was an accident.

This seemed to be enough.

"At least it wasn't yer good hand" said Anto, and they all laughed.

"Looks to me like you were in a knife fight Charlie. A lover's tiff was it?" asked Jim.

"Nothing like that" I said.

The clock on the wall said it was eleven, but I felt wide awake.

"I have a bottle of scotch in my room" I volunteered.

I don't know why I said that.

Maybe it was because I felt the need to bond with these men.

"You're a good boy Charlie" said Jim. "Go fetch it, will ya?"

So I did.

Brian decided we needed music.

There was a record player next to the television and a handful of LPs in their sleeves.

Among the albums there was one by Jim Reeves and one by Simon and Garfunkel.

Brian put on Bridge Over Troubled Water first.

He had elected himself to be in charge of music.

"Will ye ever put some clothes on Jimbo?" asked Anto.

"I will not" he said. "Am I getting ye all hard Anto? Is that it?"

"Feck off Jim" replied Anto.

Jim only had to give Anto a look and the message was clear.

No one tells Jimbo to fuck off!

In a strange kind of a way I think this is why Jim took to me.

I appeared to be a very polite young man, and I certainly wasn't going to be swearing at Jim.

I was going to do my very best not to offend him in any way.

Surely his comrades must know this by now!

As if to underline this fact Jim sidled up to me and put his big arm around my shoulders.

"Why can't ye all be a bit more like Charlie boy here? You're all a bunch of offensive fuckers. Try to be a bit more feckin' polite will ya?" he said, beginning to sound exasperated.

I was pouring four glasses of scotch.

"You're a bit mean with the old whiskey Charlie" said Jim, so I doubled the measure.

"That's better" he said and took more of a swig than a sip. I'm not sure of the exact moment when I realized that it was all well out of control.

I think I must have BEGUN to realize about this time, but I wasn't about to accept it.

Jim suggested we all do another line.

I don't know how many we'd had at this stage, but it must have been about six lines each.

I was beginning to feel like my brain was about to freeze, but it was by no means unpleasant.

Anto and Brian were back at the poker table now, ready for a fresh hand.

I joined them, expecting Jim to join us.

"I bet you're wondering what else I have in the bag Charlie" he said.

"Not really" I answered truthfully.

I imagined that it might contain his wallet, (where Jim had found the credit card he used to cut the coke), and maybe some clothes.

"Have you ever seen a Glock before Charlie?" he asked.

"A glockenspiel?" I asked.

I thought his bag too small to contain a glockenspiel.

"Not a feckin' glockenspiel!" he said, laughing.

"Jimbo!" warned Anto.

"Yes Jim, leave it, will ya!" added Brian.

Jim ignored them.

"I bet the little faggot boy has never seen a feckin' gun in his life, have you Charlie?"

The truth was that I hadn't seen a gun.

I would be happy NEVER to see a gun.

Nevertheless Jim was going to show me his gun, in spite of the protests.

"Ah Jim, don't get it out now!" sighed Brian.

"Fer God's sake Jimbo!" added Anto.

"Maybe you're right" accepted Jim. "Let's play then".

It was too late.

I now knew that there was a gun in the room.

Jim had become more tactile as the night wore on.

His huge arm was always round my shoulder, and when he moved away it was never for long.

Then his big hand would soon be round the back of my neck, and then his arm would slide back round to envelope me.

This didn't make me feel safe, the way that Doc did.

It didn't arouse me the way that Al or Rob did.

Instead I felt the way that I did when my father showered me with his affections.

I felt two extremes of emotions.

On one hand it simply felt good to have affection shown to me.

On the other hand I knew where it would lead.

I was just a toy to be played with.

I still didn't feel that tired, even though I could see by the clock that it was now well past midnight.

I might not be able to sleep but I still felt it might be safer if I made my excuses and went to bed.

I yawned.

"You're NOT going to bale on us!" ordered Jim.

"Well I'm a bit tired" I told him.

"I know what will wake you up" he said, and went back to the counter to make more lines of coke.

"I'm fine" I said.

"You're NOT going to turn down our hospitality, you little faggot boy" he said.
"I don't want to take advantage Jim" I told him.
"You're not taking advantage" he told me. "You're staying".
We played poker.
Jim won the pot.
Brian and Anto seemed very unhappy about that.
I didn't understand.
We weren't playing for money.
We were just using chips.
"Are you sure you didn't mark the cards Jimbo?" asked Brian.
Jim glared at Brian, who went to the stereo and put on a Led Zeppelin album.
"I'm takin' a bath" Brian announced, leaving the record to play.
"Don't wash it too hard" laughed Jim.
Brian left the room, and seconds later I heard the taps running.
This left only me, Jim and Anto in the room.
"Another game" said Jim.
"Not for me" said Anto. "I can't afford the stake anymore".
I was obviously missing something.
There was no stake.
These were just chips.
I didn't understand.
Jim explained.
"Ya see this chip with the number one on it?" he asked.
I did, of course.
"To us that means a hundred notes. Do ye follow?" he asked me.
No I didn't.

As far as I was concerned I wasn't playing for money.
I had no money.
"And these ones with the number ten on it. To us they're a thousand notes. I figure these boys owe me about fifty thousand each by now" he laughed heartily.
I frowned.
"Don't you be worrying Charlie, you were never part of this" he clarified. "Not in that way. Sure, why should we try to be takin' money off YOU?"!
I was relieved.
He gave me a hug.
He let go of me for a second, winked at me, then headed back to the counter.
He cut a few more lines and snorted one.
He offered me another.
I didn't want another line.
I didn't need a line.
I took the line because I felt bullied into it.
That's the truth.
There was nothing I could do.
"What do you think of this Charlie?"
Jim had put a hand into his sports bag.
Ant made a sound as if he was against what Jim was about to do, but it was too late.
Jim pulled out a large hunting knife.
I might never have seen a gun before but I had seen knives. This one was impressive, although I wasn't really in the mood for knives right now, especially after being wounded by one so recently.
"It's a proper knife isn't it Charlie?" he said, waving it from side to side like he was a martial arts expert, which he may well have been, thinking about it.
He twirled it, and swapped it from one hand to the other.

I noticed how well toned his pectoral muscles were.
They bounced and rippled with every movement.
Jim might well be overweight, but underneath that extra
weight was pure muscle.
I wondered how a man might gain so much muscle.
I had a sudden vision of Jim, in a prison gym, spending
years honing his body, because there was nothing else to
do.
Countless squats had built his calf muscles and quads to
mammoth proportions.
Only the heaviest of weights could have created arms and
chest like that.
I noticed for the first time how short Jim was.
Far from making him seem less powerful I knew it made
him more dangerous because he would have a low centre
of gravity.
He shared this quality with my father.
I don't know why I said it but these words came out of my
mouth.
"You're a lot like my father" I told him.
"Was he a cunt like me Charlie?" Jim grinned.
I don't know why Jim's words had such a huge effect on
me.
Jim wouldn't have known the effect of his words.
I found myself trying to hold back a flood of tears.
"I don't think you're a cunt Jim" I said.
"Well said" Jim told me, patting me on the back, still
holding a knife in his other hand.
Anto was still waiting at the poker table.
I guess he was still there because he hadn't been dismissed.
Anto was looking at Jim's boxer shorts, I could see.
I followed Anto's gaze.
Jim's meaty penis was hanging out of the gap at the front.

Anto was shaking his head.

"Will ya ever put yer feckin' Mickey away, Jim. It's feckin' disgustin'!"

Jim looked at me and said

"I've had enough of this cunt"

Then he ordered me to

"Sit the fuck down Charlie", which I did without question.

Then, in what seemed like a single movement, Jim stepped behind Anto and then slit his throat from ear to ear with the hunting knife.

The first spurt of blood hit me full in the face and chest, covering me.

Anto grabbed at the slice in his throat trying to stop the gush of blood.

I could hear the wheezing of breath as Anto gasped his last breaths through the gap in the flesh of his neck.

I was immobile and speechless with shock.

Anto's limp body slumped to the table, where it fell on the last cards. There was no doubt that Anto was dead.

Then Jim calmly went back to the counter.

I should have run for my life at that moment but I was in shock.

Jim rummaged in his sports bag, pulling out his gun; the Glock!

He sat back down in his seat, pointing the gun at me, but still brandishing the bloody knife, almost ceremoniously.

"I bet your Da never did THAT!" laughed Jim.

I knew by now that this wasn't a conversation.

"Now Charlie, my little faggot boy, get your skinny carcass over here. You're going to give your daddy a good time."

Jim was till pointing the gun at me, and I was certain it had to be loaded.

Even if there had been NO gun, pointing at me, I already knew the damage that Jim could do with a knife.

Jim was stronger than me and he was probably faster, in spite of his mass.

Jim dropped his boxers and then forced me round to his side of the table.

He slammed the hunting knife onto the table with a loud clap.

He now grabbed my hair tightly in one hand.

He sat down on the dining chair, and then forced my face into his crotch.

"Suck it Charlie boy" he said.

The gun was pointed at my skull.

I sucked his thick penis and within seconds he was fully erect.

He rocked my head back and forth.

He took my good hand and made me play with his balls, all the time he was laughing and moaning with pleasure.

"Don't you worry Charlie boy. Just keep your daddy happy, and nothing bad will happen to ye".

I was suddenly five years old again, in a toilet cubicle, at the seaside.

The five year old Charlie did nothing, only sucked and played with daddy's balls.

Jim Watson had taught me how, by putting a finger up his arse, it would be a more intense climax.

It was usually quicker too.

I thought I might risk putting a finger up Jim Fox, in the hope of speeding up his orgasm.

While still sucking and playing with Jim's balls I used one finger to explore his hole.

"Ah, ya good thing ya" he moaned, and I knew this was going to work.

He pushed my hand further into him.

All the time that the gun was pointing at my head I knew I was relatively safe.

I doubted Jim would pull the trigger and risk shooting off his own cock.

He caressed my face with his gun, as if this would arouse me somehow.

I was petrified with fear.

A decade of abuse had desensitized me to the sex itself.

I was only thinking of how to get out of this alive.

I had every reason to believe that Jim was so coked up and drunk on spirits that he'd kill me with knife or gun, just as soon as I'd serviced him.

If I was going to die like this then I was going to make this blowjob a good one.

If I made this the best blow job of Jim's life then I figured I might just survive.

The rocking movements came faster.

His moans became louder.

"Swallow every drop Charlie, like a good faggot boy" he whispered.

I could hear the bathroom door open.

I hoped against hope that Brian might find a way to rescue me from this.

Even as I thought this I knew it was in vain.

Jim had all the weaponry.

Brian came in through the living room door at that moment, (wearing just a towel), and his eyes widened as he surveyed the scene.

He took it all in; Jim and me, Anto's slumped head, the blood.

"What the fuck!" he said.

Brian made as if to run, but Jim had seen and heard him.

Jim fired the gun, two shots one after the other, which both hit home.

Brian fell to the floor.

"Keep going Charlie" Jim ordered, without losing a stroke.

My finger massaged Jim's hole, while my other fingers stroked his balls.

I sucked him the way my father had taught me to suck.

I enveloped the entire dick with my mouth, sliding up and down the shaft, using my tongue as an extra stimulus, making unexpected movements with it, teasing him to orgasm.

"If you're good Charlie I might keep you. Would you like that?" he asked.

I couldn't speak, but I made a moan, as if to say 'yes daddy I'd like that'.

His moaning and rocking were frantic now and I knew it wouldn't be long before he came.

What would happen after that I had no idea.

There was no one to rescue me now.

Stairway to Heaven was playing on the stereo: it was the guitar solo.

I thought it might not be long before I would see Heaven now.

"Swallow it Charlie" moaned Jim. "You swallow every last drop like a good boy. Do you hear me?"

I moaned a reply.

I could taste salt and there was extra moisture in my mouth.

I knew it wouldn't be long now.

I tasted Jim's pre-cum.

His body stiffened and he went into spasm preparing for the orgasm.

I was ready to swallow as I'd been instructed, but I figured that RIGHT NOW would be my only chance.

Mentally I worked out the route to the front door, taking into account Brian's body on the floor.

No, I thought. I would need more of an advantage than this.

Jim's orgasm wouldn't be enough to slow him down.

His boxers were on the floor where they'd been dropped. With my wounded hand I wrapped his boxers around his ankles.

I hoped that he would be too busy coming and that he didn't notice me fussing with his underwear.

Or, if he DID notice, maybe he thought I had a fetish for feet and ankles.

I hoped that if he tried to chase after me he might trip over his boxers and fall.

Before that, though, I'd have to dodge bullets, and maybe a thrown knife.

For some reason I thought I might be able to run out of here using a side to side movement, tacking like sailors did, against the wind.

I might dodge bullets that way, I hoped.

It was too late now in any case.

He was coming now and he held onto my hair too tightly, so escape wasn't an option.

"Swallow Charlie" he ordered.

There was a spurt in my mouth and then another.

Each spurt was matched by a shaking in Jim's body.

Jim was spent now, and I knew my end was near.

I wouldn't see the morning.

Jim loosened the tight grip on my hair and began to stroke it instead.

"You're a good boy Charlie" he said.

Robert Plant was singing 'And she's buying a stairway to Heaven', ending the song.

"Do you want me to be your daddy, Charlie?" Jim asked me.

He was looking me in the eyes.

I knew it was a serious question.

"Yes Jim" I told him.

I was on the verge of tears and maybe Jim thought I was being sincere.

I only wanted to live to see another day, but if Jim believed me then that was all to the good.

"Good" he said.

He let me go now, but still had his gun aimed at me as if he wasn't completely sure about me.

"I want to trust you Charlie, I really do. How am I going to trust you?"

I didn't know and shook my head.

"We'll think of something" he said, and he looked round at the mess of bodies.

He made a tutting sound and pushed himself up from the chair.

He nearly tripped over the boxers I'd had ravelled about his ankles.

'Damn' I thought, 'maybe I could have run for it after all', but it was too late now.

He went to the counter, with his boxers still about his ankles, and put the bag of coke into his sports bag.

There were still a few lines left on the counter.

He snorted one and then handed me the note he'd just used.

"Have a line Charlie boy" he ordered.

He pulled up his boxers while I took a line.

The coke only made me more frightened somehow.

I began to shake.

I looked at Anto and Brian and I was almost sick at the destruction of human life.

Jim saw me looking at the bodies.

"Don't you be getting sad about them, they were cunts. I wanted rid of them anyway. You should have been lying there with them, by all accounts!"".

He looked me up and down, shaking his head.

"What am I going to do with you Charlie?"

All I could think was 'please let me live, please let me live'.

He raised his gun and pointed it me.

Then he pointed the gun away from me, towards the floor.

Having thought about it for a second or two it seemed Jim had decided on a course of action.

"Change your T-shirt" he said. "And put on a warm jacket."

He followed me to my room.

I had a notion that Jim might leave me alone in my room while I changed.

I thought I might use that moment to climb out of the window and run.

That wasn't going to happen though.

Jim followed me into the room, still carrying with him his sports bag.

I found a clean T-shirt, changed into it.

Then I put on a jacket.

"Come with me" he said.

He herded me to his room.

He closed the door behind us.

He stood by the door and ordered me to fetch him some clothes.

He made me stand at the other side of the room, by his window.

I looked at the window, hopefully, but I knew that as long as Jim had the gun there really was no hope.

Somehow he managed to dress while still holding a gun on me.

"This wasn't supposed to happen this way" he said.

I tried to think of a way to make him trust me.

I figured that if he trusted me enough then he might put the gun away.

He might take his eyes off me for a moment and I could make my escape.

I realized something about cocaine now.

It had the ability to clarify thought.

I knew that in Jim's case it also had the power to push a person right over the edge.

I had a feeling that Jim wasn't a stranger to nights like this.

I wondered how many men he had killed before.

I guessed it had to be a fair few.

I didn't think it was possible to kill so casually without a bit of practice.

"I know you don't trust me yet Jim" I told him. "But you CAN trust me. I WANT you to trust me. You're a lot like my dad, in so many ways Jim, you KNOW I'm not lying, don't you?"

Jim took a few seconds to look me straight in the eye.

"I DO believe you Charlie boy, but that doesn't mean I can trust you, not yet anyway".

"I know you can't trust me just yet Jim, but we BOTH of us want you to be able to trust me".

I could see he was trying to understand me.

"So what are ye sayin'?" he asked.

"I'm not really sure, but suppose I come with you. Suppose you make it so I can't leave you. I don't know how. Tie me up so I can't run off or something" I suggested.

"Good thinkin' Charlie. I don't WANT to tie you up, but it might be for your own good. Is that okay?" he said, and there was concern in his voice, which was weird after all that had happened.

"It'll be fine Jim" I said.

He thought about it all for a minute.

"I'm going to need you to help with Anto and Brian. Can you do that?" he asked.

"Sure" I told him.

He put the gun in the waistband of his jeans and he walked me back towards the living room, still carrying his sports bag.

"You should be lyin' here dead" he said sadly, "instead of these eejits!"

There, in the doorway, was Bryan's body.

The towel had fallen off him, exposing his buttocks.

"My God Jim" I said. "He's still breathing."

Jim pulled the gun from his waistband, ready to finish off what he'd started.

"No Jim, please don't" I begged.

Jim had the gun in his hand and aimed.

Then he pointed the gun away.

Then he pointed the gun back at Brian's still breathing body.

His hand stayed in the position for a moment, shaking a little.

Then he put the gun back in his waistband.

"Fuck" he said. "Fuck! Fuck! Fuck""

He kicked Brian in the chest, and Brian moaned.

I bent down to see what I could do for Brian.

One bullet, I could see had passed right through the flesh at his shoulder.

There was a lot of blood but I could see it was only a flesh wound.

I looked for the other bullet wound.

I could see a trickle of blood where Brian's left ear met his skull.

It was just a graze, but maybe it had been enough to knock him unconscious.

"He'll live" I said.

I could see that Jim didn't think this was an advantage.

"Okay, okay. Brian I can deal with" Jim said.

We looked across at Anto.

"Right" he said with purpose. "We get Anto in the back of the van".

Anto was a large man.

Only just a man really, regardless of his size.

He should have had a long life ahead of him.

Jim put his sports bag back onto the counter-top, then took Anto by the arms, the head flopped back and hole in his neck was suddenly the size of a dinner plate, and I carried him by the legs.

We took Anto out to the back of the white van that was parked there and threw him in.

I was still trying to find the chance to escape.

I knew there'd be only one chance, if that.

It wasn't going to be right now though.

Jim held me close to him, making me walk in front, and we walked back into the guest house.

Where Brian's body had been there was just his towel.

Jim was suddenly in a frenzy.

He had his gun in his hand now, but he had let me go.

At that moment I had my back to Jim, but I stepped away and looked back at him.

Right behind him I could see Brian, raising the hunting knife, plunging it into Jim's back.

Jim screamed an animal scream, fell forward, turning as he fell.

He fired a shot at Brian in mid-fall, which this time hit the heart.

In one moment blood was spurting out of Brian and onto me, and at the same time Jim had fallen on the knife that was in his back pushing it further in so that the blade now protruded from his chest.

Jim's blood spurted onto me as well.

Once again I had been covered in blood, but this time by two different men.

They were both dead.

I sat on the floor almost collapsing onto it, knowing that I really SHOULD do something now, but for the life of me I couldn't think.

Then there was the strangest thing.

I could smell the distinctive scent of lavender.

Jim's body was right there in front of me.

I didn't know what to feel.

Seeing him lying there, looking so much like my father, I was filled with so many mixed emotions.

The strongest of all those emotions, I'm ashamed to say, was grief.

After the longest while I decided that the best thing would be to drive the white van down to the main house.

I would wake up Mary and Doc, (please God Agnes had been well sedated because I didn't want to see her).

They would know what to do next.

I found the van keys in Jim's jeans pocket.

Then I drove the quarter mile back to the main house.
I knocked on the door and a light went on.
Mary answered the door and saw I was covered in blood.
"Oh my God!" she said. "What on earth has happened?"
I couldn't explain.
I told her to call the police.
Doc appeared from nowhere.
"What's happened? Are you okay?"
He'd seen the blood and thought it must be mine.
I tried my best to explain but I knew that it would seem too
incredible, especially after Agnes stabbing me.
I was sure it would appear that I was determined to repeat
patterns of stabbings, blood and death.
Agnes was suddenly there.
She was in a gossamer-like night gown with a lace shawl
wrapped around her.
"Get him OUT of here!" she screamed.
Mary tried to keep her away from me.
"He is EVIL! Get him out!"
Mary had to ignore Agnes in the end.
She guided me to the kitchen, Doc at my side.
Then she closed the door on Agnes, keeping it shut with a
chair at the handle.
"I called the police" Mary said.
"I think I should go up to the guest house to see if there's
something I can do" said Doc.
I wasn't so sure this was a good idea.
"Even so" he said. "I want to make sure there's nothing to
incriminate you up there. I only want to do what's best".
I told him there were dead bodies up there.
There was a sports bag with coke in it up there.
What was he going to do?
Contaminate the crime scene!

Agnes was still screaming madly at the kitchen door as the police arrived.

Now, though, she was screaming, "Murderer! Killer!"

I already knew that I would have a difficult time explaining everything without any help from Agnes.

I didn't know how difficult it was going to be.

I was soon to find out.

Chapter Six

Two uniformed policemen questioned me initially, in Mary's kitchen.

I must have seemed incoherent because they made me go over the story a few times.

Doc was with me throughout, but Mary had escorted Agnes back to her room, and then kept her there.

One of the policemen went up to the guest house to verify my story.

Within half an hour the place was overrun with police.

I was taken to the police station for further questioning, where I repeated my story.

I had the feeling that I wasn't believed but what could I do? I could only tell the truth.

A plain clothes officer, by the name of Behan, told me I was under arrest for the suspected murder of three men whose names I had never heard before.

There was a Michael, and a Liam, and an Eamonn.

There was no mention of Jim, Anto or Brian.

I guessed that they'd all given me false names.

Behan read me my rights and told me I'd spend the night in a holding cell.

Before being taken to the cell I was asked to give blood so it could be tested.
I dreaded to think what they'd find in my blood.
Valium, the medication the doctor had given me, alcohol.
It was enough.
I also needed to provide them with fingerprints.

I found myself in a small cell.
Claustrophobia descended on me now and I became frantic.
I forced myself to take deep breaths.
I thought about Scout and how I might never see him again.
I thought of all my loved ones, especially Doc, and I prayed that he might believe me enough to get me out of here.
I imagined that if I was convicted of a triple murder I might not be free for decades.
My mind went down every avenue, but every one was a dead end.
I tried to sleep, only to find myself in a panic.
Then I would try to calm myself enough to fall asleep again.
Sleep still avoided me, and the whole cycle began again.

In the morning Behan took me from my cell to an interview room where I was questioned yet again.
"It seems that you have a history of mental illness" Behan said.
"I wouldn't say that" I told him.
"Well, you tell me how you would describe it then?"
"I was under a lot of stress and suffered a nervous breakdown, once!" I explained.

"And how is that different form mental illness?" he asked.
"Well firstly I don't think it shows a HISTORY of mental illness. It was ONE single episode. And secondly, I'm not sure that what I suffered could really be described as a mental illness".
"So, how would you describe it?"
I could feel the walls closing in on me.
"Look, I did nothing wrong. I was the victim" I shouted.
Behan was unmoved.
"Tell me how you hurt your hand" he said.
I explained the best I could.
"So, if I understand right then you were attacked but didn't come to the police? That doesn't seem feasible, does it?"
"Feasible or not, that's how it happened" I said, getting more desperate.
Behan was reading through his notes and said nothing.
"Look" I said. "Surely you're going to check to see if my prints are on any of the weapons?"
"The results will be back in a few hours" he said, but didn't take his eyes off the notes he was still reading.
"It says here that, just before he was murdered, Liam Coleman had ejaculated. He had been involved in a sexual encounter. Can you throw any light on that?"
"I think that must be Jim. Jim Fox he called himself" I began my difficult explanation.
"Go on".
"He held a gun to my head and made me give him a blowjob".
Behan raised an eyebrow.
"And Eamonn Miller was found missing all his clothes. Is that significant?"
"He'd just come out of the bath".
I could hear that my voice was high pitched and whining.

"We found a substantial amount of cocaine. Did you have anything to do with that?" he asked.

"These guys virtually bullied me to try the stuff. I never did it in my life before last night, I swear".

"A substantial amount of money was found; about three thousand pounds. What do you know about that?"

I didn't know anything about any money.

Whichever way I looked at it they were building up a strong case against me.

"Let me explain this to you. Every word of what you say seems so improbable, when what seems more likely is that this is some kind of drug deal gone wrong. Add to this that there's some sort of homosexual element going on. Are you homosexual?" he asked.

"Well, as it happens, yes I am, but that has nothing to do with anything".

"It seems more likely that you were under stress. Maybe, because of your history of mental illness, and your homosexuality, fuelled by cocaine, (and, by all accounts a fair amount of alcoholic spirits), together with medication you had only just been given, something inside you just snapped. Doesn't that seem more likely than the story you've been telling?"

"But I'm telling you the truth" I repeated.

"I don't think you were in a fit state to know the truth" he said.

I wondered if there was the slimmest possibility that I had imagined the entire thing. Maybe I had reprogrammed my memory because what I had done was too horrible to contemplate.

I was stunned to silence.

"Perhaps the results of the prints will tell us more clearly what happened. We'll know by this afternoon. Until then

you'll remain in your cell. If the results are returned but they don't back up your story, then you will be held here, in a holding cell until a preliminary hearing is arranged. You can expect a preliminary hearing to be held in the next day or two. And if it goes to the preliminary hearing we will stress that we believe you to be a flight risk, and ask for bail to be denied. If, after that, you are found guilty in a court of law, we will demand the severest of sentences".
I was still silent. There was nothing more I could say.
"Do you understand the seriousness of your situation?"
I told him I did.
He escorted me back to my cell.

I wondered what my life would be like in prison.
Perhaps it wouldn't be so bad.
I tried to look on the bright side but I found myself at one dead end after another.
I thought that if I could just cut myself, just once, then I might find a solution.

Time passed by slowly in that cell.
The walls closed in on me.
I prayed that the results would show that I was telling the truth; that I hadn't touched a single one of the weapons.
I tried to recall now.
Had I touched the gun, just once?
What about the knife?
Had I laid a hand on it at any time?
I couldn't remember it very well now.

I was back in time now.
I was with Jim.
He aimed his gun at Brian while he lay on the floor.
He hesitated, and didn't fire.

Suppose he HAD fired.

Jim would still be alive now.

I would still be his captive, but I would be free compared to this living hell.

We would have put Brian's body in the back of the van, next to Anto.

Then I would have allowed Jim to tie me up, because he still couldn't trust me.

I would be a captive, and terrified.

But it would have been better than THIS.

I tried to remember.

Had I begged Jim NOT to fire the gun into Brian's prone body?

I thought that perhaps I HAD begged him, but I couldn't be sure.

If I had begged Jim NOT to shoot, and Jim didn't shoot because I had begged him, then it was my own fault I was here right now.

I surely only had myself to blame.

And what had my begging achieved anyway? Brian was still dead, and now Jim was too.

I felt sick.

This was just another dead end.

The locks in the cell door clunked and Behan now stood in the open doorway.

"You're free to go" he said simply.

I sat where I was, on the edge of my bunk, unable to move.

"Didn't you hear me? You're a free man."

I still couldn't believe it, not really.

Even so, I rose from the bunk and followed Behan out of the cell.

"We may still need you to help with our inquiry if there's a case to be brought. You may need to make yourself available pending such an inquiry. I would also suggest that you don't speak to the press Mr Watson, until any inquiry is concluded."

"Am I free to leave the country?" I asked.

"As I said, you are a free man. But in the event, we may need you to return".

I thanked him and soon I found myself in the main reception area, where I saw Doc. I was never so pleased to see him as I was then.

I hugged him uncontrollably and tears flowed more freely now than at any time before.

"It's all over now Charlie" he said.

We got into the hire car.

"Where are we going?" I asked.

"My aunt's!" he replied

"I can't go back there Doc. Drop me off at a hotel or something. I'm not going back there".

He understood, I think.

I couldn't face Mary, and I certainly wasn't prepared for another onslaught from Agnes.

He drove us to a hotel where he booked us both in.

Then we went up to our room.

He wanted to hear everything but he knew I wasn't ready.

All I knew was that I needed a proper sleep in a good bed, not a cell bunk.

I'd be able to talk to him later.

I was still covered in dried blood, but I didn't care right now.

I laid down on the big bed.

Doc soothed my frown.

He promised me that he'd be back before I knew it.

Doc, as he'd promised, was back at my side within a few hours.

He'd packed up all our belongings and made our apologies to Mary.

Agnes, Doc told me, was still in a hysterical state, and it looked like she might have to be sectioned.

He hinted that it might not be her first time, that she may well have been sectioned at least once before.

Our return ticket wasn't for another two weeks.

We decided we should take advantage of our time here and see a bit of the country.

Our first destination, we thought, could be the Giant's Causeway.

Beyond that we made no plans.

We would take it one day at a time.

We were in the city of Newry I discovered.

We were staying at the Canal Court Hotel.

We didn't venture beyond its walls.

We ate in its restaurant and then drank in the bar.

Very slowly I began to tell Doc everything that had happened, but some parts of the story were more difficult to relate than others.

"None of this would have happened if I'd been there" he said. "If not for Agnes and her hysterics all this might have been prevented".

I wasn't of the same mind.

The entire series of events had a feeling of being choreographed, at least I saw it that way.

I told Doc about the carved knife I had found in the wood that time (so long ago in my memory now).

I told him about the smell of lavender.

I even told him about my dream when Peter the handsome sang to me;
Daddy's going to be your valentine.
He listened attentively, but how much he believed I wasn't so sure.
The thing Doc thought was the most significant was that Liam Coleman had chosen to call himself Jim Fox.
Doc believed that, had I not had all those terrible experiences with Jim Watson in my youth, then I would most likely be dead now.
I wouldn't have been in any way prepared for what was to happen; had it all only happened last night?
"Another thing" Doc said.
I was listening, but I was reaching the point now when all I wanted to do was put it behind us.
"I don't know how significant it is. You said your mother handed Peter a plate of lamb?"
"That's right, he did".
"Did you know that Agnes means 'lamb'?"
It hadn't occurred to me.
I wasn't sure of the significance either.
Maybe it would all become clear.
"Do you still have that feeling of dread?" he asked.
I meditated on that for a moment.
"Do you know something? It's gone! There's no more feeling of dread!" I told him.
"So do you think it was a premonition?" he wondered.
"Doc, what good is a premonition? It can't change anything".
"Maybe so, but that's not what I asked. Whether a premonition is any good or not, whether it can change anything or not; they're all beside the point. Do you think it was a premonition?"

I told him that I thought perhaps it was.

"Just promise me that next time you get a premonition, or a feeling of dread, you tell me. We'll vanish to Hawaii for three months".

I promised him.

"Mind you" I added, "the premonition might be about Hawaii, and all we've done is travel there sooner. I don't think we can escape our destiny. If there's even such a thing. I'm not even sure you can postpone it. All you can do, maybe, is dodge it at the last minute".

"Well you certainly did that!" he said.

I laughed for the first time then.

I couldn't even remember the last time.

Then I remembered the last time I laughed.

"We're the bad guys" Jim had said. "The ones your mammy warned you about".

I had laughed at that.

I recalled a small detail.

Somewhere along the line I had made a promise to remove my blindfold and really SEE what was going on around me.

I was sure that the reason all these things happened to me was because I walked through life wearing a blindfold.

I remembered now.

Doc's mother. There was some kind of a mass for her. Was I remembering correctly?

I asked him.

"Yes" he said. "That's supposed to be today, but I won't be going, not after all that's happened."

"You should really go. Don't worry about me" I told him.

"What would you do if I decided to go?"

"I don't know. Have a bit of a wander maybe".
"Well, don't wander far. I won't be long".

Doc went to his mother's mass.
I had no doubt that Mary and Agnes would be there.
It wasn't my place to be part of their event.
I felt it was important that Doc went though.
It was the start of me taking the blindfold off.
I promised myself I would ask Doc about his mother.
I wanted to know how she died.
I wanted to know how young Doc would have been.
Doc knew so much about the trauma I had been through, both recent and distant.
Wasn't it only right that I find out about the things that made him tick?
I decided that I would be more supportive when it came to his son, Nicholas.
It was ridiculous that I didn't even know how old he was.
Until very recently I had been busy, although that was not a valid excuse.
I wasn't busy now.
I would make an effort.
I decided that, for the rest of our stay on this beautiful island, I would get to know as much as I could about the man I loved.

When Doc got back from the mass I tried to judge how easy it was going to be drawing him out.
I wondered why he seemed so unemotional considering he'd been to his mother's grave.
Perhaps he only APPEARED to be unemotional, and that appearance was covering up great pain.
I figured that this must be the case.

"How did the mass go?" I asked.

I wasn't about to start walking on eggshells.

I would be gentle, but I wouldn't be afraid of broaching a subject if it meant getting closer to Doc.

"Considering what else we've been through recently it was a walk in the park" he said.

"How do you feel?" I asked him.

"Fine" he said, and he sounded quite happy. "I was more concerned about you being on your own here."

"Well that's weird, because all I was thinking about was YOU".

It was the truth.

We were about to spend the next two weeks together.

We had never spent so much time alone with each other.

I didn't need to know absolutely everything all in one go.

We could take it slow.

I told him my plan.

I told him I wanted to take my blindfold off and start to get to know him properly.

For a second he looked horrified.

He quickly changed his expression, but just for a second he really looked horrified.

Or was I imagining that brief look of his?

No, I was certain.

It was there, if just for a split second.

This was the proof then; that he was hiding so much pain, and the thought of revealing it horrified him.

As if to confirm my theory he said,

"Everything is fine between us Charlie. Really. Everything has ALWAYS been fine between us".

"It's just that sometimes it feels like a one way street. You're always there for me, but I'm not there for you. I know nothing about how your mother died, or what she looked like, or any of that," and Doc didn't let me finish; he interrupted me.

"But you don't need to know what she looked like!"

"That seems unfair when you have a picture of my stepfather!" I argued.

Doc thought about this for a second.

"I'm sure I can lay hands on a photo, if that's what you want".

I shook my head slightly.

Considering he was such an intelligent man he could also be very slow.

"I told you lots of stuff about me Doc; the abuse, my cutting myself, my breakdown. You were there for me when my dog died. You're here for me now, after this nightmare triple killing. You've told me very little about your stuff! When I have been there for anything in your life? All I've ever done is be there for your 'Turning Point' as you call it." I said as calmly as I could.

"Well that's all I've needed you for. My life isn't a series of dramas" he said.

I felt like saying to him, "you mean like MY life is a series of dramas".

Although I FELT like saying it I didn't say it.

Doc had only said what he'd said because it was true.

HIS life wasn't a series of dramas.

He wasn't trying to tell me that MINE was.

Although, actually, my life really WAS a series of dramas, if I thought about it.

I laughed quietly.

"What are you laughing about?" he asked me inquisitively, without agenda.

"I was thinking that you're with me now. It won't be long before your life IS a series of dramas".

He laughed too.
That was good.
At least we still had that.
We could still laugh.
I repeated to Doc what I'd been thinking while he was at the mass.
"There's no hurry anyway Doc. We have two weeks together, and if we haven't split up by then, who knows?" There was that same flicker of terror, just for a split second, then it was gone.
He recovered.
"True" he said. "There's no hurry".
I couldn't wait. Soon I would be seeing things the way they really are; without a blindfold.

Chapter Seven

During the Second World War there was an American army base close to the village where Doc's mother and her sister Mary grew up.
One wouldn't need psychic powers to predict that the pretty young woman and an army base full of virile young men might end in a pregnancy.
The young man in question went to war and never came back.
The pretty young woman soon had a child, but wasn't strong enough to be able to carry the shame of it all.
She committed suicide when the boy was only a few months old.
The boy, named Desmond, had an older cousin called Agnes who became more of a sister when his aunt Mary decided to raise him as her own.

Mary raised the boy as best she could but Desmond soon found himself in trouble with the law, on more than one occasion.

Music had been his saviour.

When the boy was eighteen he decided he would try to find relatives on his dead father's side, (after whom he was named).

He found them on the other side of the Atlantic and moved closer to be with them.

At university he met and fell in love with Sandra, who gave him a son Nicholas, (now aged ten).

This is what I discovered about Doc during the two weeks we toured Ireland.

Doc agreed we would meet Sandra when we returned home, but I could see that he really didn't want to introduce me as his lover.

He preferred to introduce me as a friend, student, and house mate.

I said that I had no problem with that.

I understood that Doc and Sandra had raised a family together.

Of course he'd feel uncomfortable telling her he was now in a relationship with me.

Doc and I had spent a week driving round The coast of Ireland, from Coleraine, to Galway, then on to Tralee and Cork. From there we drove to Wexford and reached Dublin.

We had another three or four days left of our holiday.

I suggested a trip to Newgrange, as Bette had once described.

It really WAS reminiscent of a manger.

Having seen all there was to see we returned to Dublin.

Here we did all the things tourists are expected to do. We saw the Book of Kells, visited Kilmainham Jail. We spent a day in Phoenix Park and saw herds of deer.

We looked at shop windows in Grafton Street and George Street. We ate in a restaurant in Dame street. We drank in a pub called the Brazen Head, reputedly the oldest in Ireland.

Our barman asked us if we were on holiday.

We said that we were.

He winked at us as he told us that there were only two types of people in the world.

"The Irish, and the ones who WANT to be Irish" he explained with a laugh.

By now we were both getting used to the Irish humour and spirit.

We loved it here, but soon it would be time to fly home.

Our hotel was situated right on the quays and faced onto the River Liffey.

From our window we had the best view of the skyline, which was a festival of green domes, brown chimneys and spires.

Our phone rand and Doc answered.

"It's for you" he said, and handed me the phone.

I made a face, as if to say 'who could this be?'

"Hello" I said.

"Mr Watson?" came a strident male voice with a Northern Irish accent.

"Yes" I confirmed.

"This is Mick O'Brien from the Newry Reporter. I want to speak to you about an incident I'm reporting on, which I believe you were involved in", he said.

"I'm sorry Mr O'Brien. I'm afraid I can't help you. The police told me not to speak to the press until the matter has been resolved."

"I see. In which case, perhaps I can speak to you AFTER the case has been resolved, and get your story THEN?"

I didn't see why not.

"Sure" I said.

"Could you give me a number where I can reach you," he asked.

I told him I didn't feel comfortable doing that.

I said I would feel more comfortable if he gave me HIS number.

I took his number down and promised to call.

Doc didn't look happy about this exchange.

When I'd put the phone down he said;

"I don't think you should be speaking to those people!"

"Sure" I said, "but you can see it would make a great story, and the guy is just doing his job".

Doc grunted something unintelligible.

I took my Valium in preparation for the flight.

Even though I had recently narrowly escaped death, (at Jim Fox's hand), I was still morbidly afraid of flying.

I should have realized that if my life had been spared once then it was for a reason. I was certainly NOT meant to die in a plane crash!

We were back, in our new home. Roger had looked after it for us while we were away.

I was in no doubt he'd thrown a few parties.

I figured he might even have invited a few girls back.

He seemed happy to see us, as we were happy to see him.

I told him about the 'adventure' as I'd begun to call it.

He was open-mouthed with shock and disbelief.

Doc and I collected Scout from my parents.
They didn't know we'd even been away.
They thought we had spent a fortnight moving and decorating.
They didn't need to know.
News had reached these shores about an incident in County Down, a triple murder, but no one had connected it with us. My name wasn't mentioned, thankfully.
Scout wagged his tail and snuffled into us, trying to work out where we'd been just from our scent.
"Oh, a letter arrived for you" my mother informed me.
Knowing my mother as I did I thought it was perfectly feasible that she'd already steamed the letter open to discovered its contents. Her face told me nothing though.
I looked at the envelope.
It looked formal, as if it came from a high street bank or doctor.
"I'll open it later" I told her.
She was upset when I said that.
She wanted me to open it now.
I knew then that she hadn't steamed the letter open.
"No, we need to get back home, I'll open it later" I repeated, and we drove home.

Scout could run free in our back yard. It was fully enclosed.
There were mature trees and shrubs at the perimeter of our property and we weren't overlooked, although there were neighbours' houses on either side.

Doc and I still had a few days left where we could run free too.

Our regular routine wouldn't start up again until then.
"Did you open your letter?" Doc asked me.
I'd nearly forgotten about it.
The envelope had my previous address on it crossed out
and my mother's current address written by the side.
I opened the envelope.
It was from a firm of Brighton solicitors.
They were writing to inform me that I might have an
interest in the estate of the recently deceased Jim Watson.
I went cold as I read the letter.
The letter had been dated so I knew it had only been
posted about three weeks ago.
This would have been about the time that Jim Fox had met
his end.
I know that this would have been coincidence, but even so.
The mind makes strange links between things.
I made a note to contact the solicitors office to see what
the next step would be.

I wondered out loud if we should maybe invite Sandra
over and get to know her.
Doc was reluctant, and arranged it anyway.
Roger would be working at Harold's House so it would just
be Doc, Sandra and I.
"Would you mind being chef that night?" Doc asked me.
"Not at all" I answered.
I knew Doc wasn't really at ease in the kitchen.
"I have to warn you that Sandra likes her food" he told me.
I thought that could only be a good thing.

I roasted a chicken and potatoes, with plenty of vegetables.
I bought ice cream for dessert.
I could hear a car pull up outside.

A second later I heard a car door slam.

Feet shuffled up the wooden stairs to our front door.

Our front door bell rang.

Doc answered the door and invited Sandra in to our house.

I'd done all my preparation and was out of the kitchen and in the living room.

I was able to get my first glance of Sandra as she stepped through the front door.

The first thing to say about Sandra was that she was overweight.

She was more than just overweight; she was morbidly obese.

She wore a loose top over baggy slacks.

She had shoulder length mousey hair and glasses.

She carried a white handbag.

"Welcome to my new house" Doc was saying.

"It's lovely" she said. "And is this one of your lodgers?" she asked, looking at me.

"Lodger, friend, student" he listed. "Charlie".

"Hello Charlie" she smiled warmly.

I could see that she was once a very pretty woman, and I was instantly charmed by her.

"Hello Sandra, how are you?" I asked.

"I'm good, thanks" she said.

I could hear she was wheezing a little from climbing the eight steps that went from the ground to our front door.

"I need a cigarette" she said. "Can I smoke?"

"Of course" said Doc, and I found an ashtray.

She lit up and exhaled a stream of smoke.

I would be ready to start serving the meal now.

I made my excuse and left Sandra and Doc to talk privately, as I knew that they must.

They would need to organize times when the boy could come and visit, and Finances, and I didn't know what else. I could hear Sandra coughing, but it became quickly apparent that she coughed a lot.

"Dinner is served" I announced, grandly, and I hoped my offering would win Sandra over.

I don't know why I was so concerned about getting Sandra on my side.

I suppose I figured that if she was in Doc's life then it would make things less complicated if she and I got on. I'd roasted the chicken with garlic, lemon and butter.

I knew it was going to taste delicious with the roast potatoes and vegetables.

Sandra loved her food, as Doc had warned me.

I think I might have guessed it even without Doc's warning.

Sandra ate with the best of manners.

I don't want to suggest that she ate like a pig!

She finished off every last morsel.

I offered her second helpings and she gladly accepted.

I added to the conversation, not in huge amounts, but as if I was the seasoning to the main dish.

My part had already been played; I had met Sandra now, and she had met me.

Doc needed to organize when, and how often, his boy would be coming to stay.

"There's no doubt Desmond. The boy needs his father. He shouldn't be made to suffer just because we couldn't make our marriage work" Sandra was saying.

"How's he doing?" Doc asked her.

"He's fine. Very subdued, but then I guess that's normal. Although who knows what 'normal' really is?" she said.

"The other thing, Desmond, is that we need to talk about money!"

I knew that I had better make myself scarce.

I started to clear plates away to make space for ice-cream.

I was in the kitchen now, loading the dish-washer, and plating up ice-cream and brandy snaps.

I wasn't eaves-dropping, not deliberately.

It was happen-stance, and the acoustics of our new house, that allowed me to listen in on the conversation in the dining room.

"You missed the last four months" said Sandra.

"I was raising the deposit on this place" said Doc.

"It's a lot of money you owe me Desmond" she said.

"Thousands by now, were you aware? I know how quickly things can get out of control"

"The deposit on this place didn't leave me a lot of room for manoeuvre" he said.

"I'm sure it took a lot of arranging, but I'm not concerned with that. I just need you to start paying me regularly, or the boy suffers."

"I know, I'm sorry. I'll get right onto it" said Doc.

"It's not as if I was at fault Desmond. Really, was it?" she said.

"As you say. As you're fond of saying. I was at fault" admitted Doc.

"I didn't mean it to sound like that Desmond. It's just that I refuse to let the boy suffer, when neither of us is at fault".

I rattled glass dishes full of ice-cream and they knew I was coming back into the dining room.

They changed the subject.

We ate the ice-cream and brandy snaps, still managing to engage in polite and frothy conversation.

It seemed that I had managed to charm Sandra with my hosting skills and mammoth portions.

I poured us coffee and she lit a cigarette, coughing as she exhaled the first smoke.

"Those things will kill you Sandra" said Doc.

"You wish" she laughed.

"Not at all" Doc replied.

"Anyway, you can have the boy here every other weekend. It will be good for me to have a break actually. You have no idea what it's like to be the sole, full-time parent" Sandra was beginning to sound a bit like MY mother.

She crushed out her cigarette and shifted her large body out of the chair.

"I'd love to stay but I have to get back" she said.

She waddled over to me.

I was standing up now, as was Doc.

"Thank you Charlie, that was delicious. It was a real pleasure to meet you" she said and wrapped he arms around me.

"It's a pleasure" I said, hugging her back.

Doc escorted Sandra to her car.

She drove away and he came back into the house.

"That went well" he said to me.

I was clearing the table of all the signs of our meal.

"She seems nice" I said.

I hate using the word 'nice' but sometimes it's the only word that fits.

"Don't you mean 'fat'?" he asked.

"Well, that was a bit of a surprise. I know you warned me she might have an appetite, but I had no idea she would be so...."

"Fat!" Doc finished the sentence for me.

He sounded angry.

"While I was in the kitchen" I admitted "I could hear what you were both saying".

"Oh?" he said.

"I wasn't trying to listen in, it's just the acoustics in here" I explained.

"Okay" he accepted.

"If money is tight I can get another job" I said. "Maybe I should never have given up the Fisherman's. Maybe I can get the job back. I can speak to Barb".

"Mm, I think I have another idea" he said. "How about you become my assistant next term?"

"Are you serious?"

"Never more so. Better wages than a waiter too. What do you think?"

I could think of nothing better than to be Doc's assistant.

I had, by now, spoken to someone from the Brighton solicitors' office regarding the letter.

His name was Mr Brougham.

He was polite, yet gentle, as he informed me that I had missed the funeral.

He told me that Jim Watson had been working on the engine of his car from underneath when it had collapsed on him. He'd been rushed to hospital but his injuries were so serous that he'd died within a few hours.

Mr Brougham was sorry for my loss, but was happy to inform me that I was the sole beneficiary of the estate. Jim Watson's estate included a house, in Brighton, and savings, (or 'funds' as Brougham referred to them), of about twenty thousand pounds.

"You'll need to visit our office" said Mr Brougham "because we need your signature. Then the deeds and the funds can be transferred into your name".

I thanked him.

I knew I'd have to tell my mother that her ex-husband was now dead, and that I had inherited his wealth. If my mother had been a different woman I wouldn't have been dreading it so much. My mother, being the woman that she was and is, would turn this into her own drama and she would need to headline. I wasn't able, anymore, to play the supporting role she expected of me.

All in all I was pleased with how 'project blindfold' was going.

I knew so much more about Doc's past.

I'd met his wife, and I liked her.

She might be obese and a chain smoker, but I genuinely liked her, and I think she liked me.

I just needed to meet his boy, Nicholas.

Doc and I thought it was best if we slept apart during the boy's overnight visits.

He didn't need to know that their father had a male lover.

At about this time the Irish police contacted me.

Although I was completely in the clear, thanks to the Forensics Department, they still needed to talk to me regarding a few loose ends.

I decided I would book a flight to Dublin but break the journey at Gatwick. That way I could visit the solicitors office in Brighton.

I could give Mr Brougham the signature he needed.

I realized, by her silence on the matter, that my mother probably knew nothing about Jim Watson's death.

I wasn't going to let her know just yet.

She would only turn it into a drama about HER.

I could do without that.

I hadn't even told her about the incident in Ireland.
She wasn't aware that I'd even been away.
I wanted to keep it that way.
For now.

Nicholas was just a very ordinary boy.
If he was as bright as his parents then it wasn't obvious just yet.
I was sure he'd blossom.
He reminded me very much of myself when I was his age.
He wasn't ordinary in one sense though.
He was very subdued, especially around his father.
I was only the observer.
Once he'd been introduced to me I had hardly anything to do with him except in my role as Charlie the lodger.
I was no different to Roger the lodger.
In fact I looked to Roger to see how I should behave.
Roger was casual and naturally jolly with the boy.
He played soccer with him out the back.
I would join in.
Scout joined in too.
The one thing the boy DID love was Scout.
Even though Nick hardly spoke, unless forced, he wasn't what you would call 'sullen'.
A lot of kids, especially these days, are sullen.
They're just naturally uncommunicative and angry, feeling the world owes them something.
Nick wasn't like this.
It was as if something had broken inside of him.
I put it all down to their parents' split-up.

The first night he stayed over, (a Saturday), I had made his room as welcoming as I could.

The bedding was fresh, and there were towels and bath robes.
I was sure he'd want a bath or shower.

Doc tucked him in that first night, which left me in the piano room with Roger and Scout.
We were drinking our first beer.
"Does this mean that you're rich now?" Roger asked me.
"I guess so" I chuckled.
"You won't even IGNORE me now I suppose" he said, and I chuckled again.
Roger had harvested the plant that Mick had given me for the house warming. He'd cured the once damp leaves. It now made the perfect smoke.
He rolled a joint and I played a few chords on the piano, an E minor followed by a C major.
The chords were giving me an idea for a song.

'I can see the future,
Tomorrow's gonna be the same,
Your old name doesn't suit you,
Pick yourself a different name'.

Roger joined me at the piano, the freshly lit joint between his lips.
I'd been repeating my two chords, one chord for each bar.
He nudged me across the stool and, in perfect time, played an A minor followed by E minor.
I didn't have the words, but I sang a wordless melody over the new chords.
We laughed, knowing we'd written the beginnings of a masterpiece.
We must have been smoking, drinking, laughing and singing for about half an hour when Doc reappeared.

"Everything okay?" I asked him.

"Yep" he said. "All tucked in now".

There was a faraway look in Doc's eyes, and I figured it must feel really good to have his kid back with him, even if only for a few nights.

"Doc" I said, "I'm going to need you to tell the department I'll be away until I can sort out this thing in Ireland."

"I can do that" he said.

"And I need to sign some things for the Brighton solicitor" I added.

"It's okay" he said. "I can look after everything here while you're away. With Roger's help" he added.

"I'll help as much as I can" said Roger. "It would be a pleasure".

I knew I could completely trust Roger and Doc to look after everything while I was away.

Scout nudged me with his nose and placed a paw on my lap.

"And look after this little fella" I said. "I'm going to miss him".

"And HE'S going to miss you Charlie" Roger said.

"And I'M going to miss you too Charlie!" said Doc.

This was how I found myself flying to Gatwick airport with only a rucksack as hand luggage.

I'd discovered that if I carried only hand luggage I could bypass the long wait at the carousel and, in this case, head straight for the railway station.

Soon enough I was in Brighton, talking to Mr Brougham in his office.

I'd signed all the necessary papers.

It was only a matter of time before my father's savings, or 'funds', were transferred into my account, less tax and fees.

The house was entirely mine.

I couldn't figure out how my father had managed to buy himself a house in the few years since he'd left my mother and I.

My Brougham explained.

"You see, when you buy a mortgage you usually buy a policy, an insurance policy".

"Oh I know" I said. "I had to have a policy when we bought OUR house!"

"Well that's what happened here. Your father was insured so that in the event of his death the mortgage was paid in full."

I still couldn't believe it but I wasn't going to question it.

"And what about the savings?" I asked.

"What savings Mr Watson?" asked Brougham.

"The savings you told me about" but Brougham looked blank.

I found myself clarifying it for him.

"The money that's being transferred into my account?" I said.

"Oh, I see. No, Mr Watson" said Brougham. "That money wasn't 'savings' as such. That was also from the insurance policy".

"I guess that makes more sense" I said. "I couldn't imagine him saving that amount of money otherwise!"

Brougham offered to show me the house I now owned.

We drove to number 24 Seaview Road, which was a bungalow, slightly out of town and close to the front.

It was, indeed, a house with a sea view, as the name of the road suggested.

"What do you think you'll do with the property?"
Brougham asked, as he showed me round the place.
"I'll have to keep hold of it until I can decide. I'll probably
rent it out".
Brougham told me he could help me with the management
of the property.
That seemed like the perfect solution, to my mind.
We were in the galley kitchen and I saw a cup and other
bits of crockery and cutlery in the sink.
These must be the remains of Jim Watson's last meal.
Probably a cup of tea and a sandwich.
I felt dizzy with new emotions.
Jim Watson had been in the Royal Navy as a young man.
Naval life had taught him to keep everything 'ship-shape
and Bristol fashion'.
Apart from what I saw in the bowl, in the kitchen sink, the
house was spotlessly tidy.
Brougham showed me the garage.
Inside was a red sports car, a Jaguar.
I recognized it.
Jim had once driven me to a dogs home to pick up a
puppy.
I thought it must be the same car that had crushed my
father's body.
"This is yours" Brougham said. "As is everything else in
the house. He left you everything".
"Was there no letter or anything? Didn't he leave me some
sort of a letter with all his belongings?" I asked.
"If he did then I don't know about it. He left nothing with
me or my office as far as I know" said Brougham.
I made a decision.
"Mr Brougham, would there be anything stopping me from
staying here tonight?" I asked.

"Of course not, the house and everything in it, is yours" he answered.

"It's just I'd like to look through his belongings. Maybe he left me a note or something".

"It's possible, of course" though Brougham sounded doubtful.

I told Brougham I would drop the key off at his office the next day or two, on my way to Gatwick airport.

He bade me a polite goodbye and left me alone in Jim Watson's house.

MY house.

I went about searching for clues as to how Jim Watson had spent his later years.

I guessed he must have had friends and acquaintances.

In the front room was a sideboard with a walnut veneer.

On the sideboard were two silver frames.

Both frames contained photographs.

I recognized one of the photos.

It had been taken on one of our camping trips to Italy.

In the background was an olive grove.

In the foreground was a family group.

There were three people in the group.

On the left was my mother, wearing a sun-hat, smiling for the camera.

On the right was an image of me as a young boy of thirteen or so.

I wore a bathing suit. I looked tanned and much slimmer than I was now.

In the centre of the group was Jim Watson.

He had his huge arms around me and my mother.

He wore a pair of shorts.

He, too, was tanned with the Sorrento sun.

I wondered who had taken the picture.

Maybe it was another camper.
I tried to remember but nothing came back to me.
I realized that this was probably the same picture, or a copy of it, that my mother had given to Doc.
It was a good photo.
We all looked happy.
It's funny the things you remember.
I remembered that our camping site was called the 'Giardino Romantica'.
The romantic garden.
In the other frame was another picture of Jim Watson.
He shared the picture with a dark-haired Asian woman.
They were both in evening dress.
The picture was signed.
'To Jim, with all my love, Ruby'.
There was an 'X' underneath, symbolising a kiss.
I wondered who Ruby could be.
I continued my exploration of the house.
There was a chest of drawers in Jim's bedroom and I was looking through it now.
I found a wedding album.
It had black and white pictures of the day he married my mother.
Aside from Jim and my mother I didn't recognize as single face in these pictures.
It must have been an important memory for Jim.
Why else would he keep the album.
I was still thumbing through the wedding album.
I turned a page.
Jim had used a piece of paper as a book-mark.
On the paper was a drawing.
At the top of the paper were the scribbled words 'NEXT TATTOO?' in capitals.

It was beginning to get dark so I turned on the main light so I could better see the drawing.

It was a piece of Celtic knot-work.

The design was of a tree and at the base of the tree was the image of a dog.

I had seen this design before but couldn't remember where.

I wondered if Jim had ever managed to get this design tattooed somewhere on his body.

There was no one I could ask.

Did I really want to know?

I found that I DID want to know.

I folded the piece of paper carefully and put it into my wallet.

There was nothing else of interest in the wedding album so I closed it and put it away again.

I kept searching, hoping to find a diary, or perhaps a letter addressed to me, but there was nothing.

I found a magazine in the bottom drawer.

It was a Penthouse magazine.

Jim's porn collection!

The centrefold model was a pretty girl with curly red hair and full pink lips, called Eugenie.

For some reason I felt relieved that Jim's porn collection didn't contain sordid images of young boys.

If I found anything like that I knew I'd have to destroy those images, probably burn them.

I went into the front room again and found that the drinks cabinet contained a bottle of scotch; almost a full bottle.

I poured myself a measure.

I unfolded the sketch of Jim's tattoo and scrutinized it more closely than before.

The tree might have been an oak, but I wasn't sure.

It was intricately knotted.

I imagined it would be a painful and time consuming tattoo to execute because of its intricacy.

I looked at the base of the tree and looked at the dog.

The dog was black and had red eyes.

I thought of Duffy beneath the tree on that winter night so long ago.

Then I was suddenly reminded of the knife!

Was this the same design as the carving on the knife?

I couldn't compare one with the other.

The knife was still in the drawer of my bedside table at home.

It was getting late and I was jet-lagged. I had no idea what time my body thought it was but I was tired.

I poured myself a nightcap and decided I should go to bed.

I looked in every bedroom.

The only bed that was made up was the one in my father's bedroom.

I didn't have the energy or inclination to make up a bed so I decided I'd sleep in Jim's bed.

I put my rucksack on the bed.

I put the bedside light on.

I noticed that, by the lamp, was an ashtray.

In the ashtray was a cigarette, not yet smoked.

By the side of the ashtray was a silver lighter.

I seemed to remember now that Jim had been in the habit of placing a cigarette by his bedside, ready to smoke at the end of his day.

This cigarette, then, would have been his last cigarette of the day if he hadn't been crushed by his car.

I set my glass of scotch by the ashtray and got ready for bed.

I went to the bathroom and brushed my teeth.

I saw Jim's toiletries, among them a familiar aftershave, Tabac.

I looked in the mirrored cabinet above the sink.

There wasn't much of interest.

Some aspirin, some Preparation H in a crumpled tube, some floss, but nothing more.

I went back into the bedroom and got into the bed.

The quilt on the bed was of a green tartan, as were the pillows.

It was here that I was reminded of Jim the most.

Here was Jim's overtly masculine taste; the green tartan quilt, and the spartan décor.

Most of all, though, was his smell.

It was partly the scent of Tabac, and partly cigarette smoke.

I took a sip of my scotch, (HIS scotch, I thought).

I put his last cigarette to my lips and lit it with the silver lighter.

I tried to look at all of my emotions now, as if I could place them all under a microscope.

It might sound strange that I felt sad at Jim's passing, especially after all that had happened between us.

But I DID feel sad.

I suppose I felt most of all that there were things I needed to say to Jim but now I would never have the chance.

What things would I say to him?

I decided I would say those things to him now, in the place he had last slept.

Where his spirit might still have a chance to hear me.

I had the cigarette in one hand, and the scotch in the other.

They were like orb and sceptre in my séance ritual.

"Dad" I started.

I always addressed him as 'Dad'.
"I don't know if you can hear me. I hope you can. I believe you can. There are things I need to say to you. I need to tell you that I hated those things you did to me. Those were things that no child should ever have go through. Even so Dad, I don't hate YOU. I know that, in your way, you loved me. I need you to know that I love you too. I need you to know that I forgive you. I forgive you for everything."
Tears flowed, but I raised my glass to him in a silent toast, and drained the glass.
I took one last pull on his cigarette and stubbed it out.
Then I turned out the light.

The next morning I visited Brougham in his office.
We set up a plan for the management of the property.
This included storing Jim's Jaguar, and his other personal items, (like the wedding album).
Brougham assured me that the bungalow would be rented out in a month at the latest.
Brougham suggested I sell the Jaguar, but I couldn't bring myself to do that yet.
Although the property was in fairly good decorative order it would need some painting and decorating.
I could take a week out of my schedule and attend to that personally.
On the way back to Seaview Road I passed a tattoo parlour.
On a whim I went in.
I showed the tattooist the Celtic design.
He looked at it with admiration.
"I don't suppose it's something you would have seen before" I said to him.

"Well, it's unusual, I'll give you that! But funnily enough I had a gent come in about two or three months ago. He wanted this exact same tattoo on his back! In fact, this looks like the exact same piece of paper he gave me to work from".

He described the 'gent'.

There was no doubt that he was describing my father.

"Do you want it on your back too then?" he asked.

I hadn't planned to get tattooed at all.

I'd only come in to see if he recognized the tattoo.

It seemed he did recognize it, and knew Jim too, if only as a customer.

"How long would it take you tattoo something like this?" I asked the tattooist.

"If you want it tattooed on your back, then I could do a few hours every day for three days" he said. "And I'd only charge you twenty five quid".

"Is it painful?" I asked naively.

"Sure, but you get used to it" he soothed.

He could see I was uncertain.

"How about you go get yourself a few drinks to numb the pain and come back to me" he suggested.

I said I'd think about it.

I left the tattoo parlour.

I bought some emulsion paint and some brushes.

Once back at the bungalow I started painting the hallway.

I kept thinking about the tattoo.

Finally I decided I'd pour myself a large measure of scotch, with every intention that I'd revisit the tattoo parlour in the afternoon.

The silence, as I painted and drank, became deafening.

My imagination was playing the Kabalevsky over and over.

I looked through Jim's record collection, hoping to find something to replace the madness of the Kabalevsky.

Jim had a small collection of vinyl.

One of his albums was something I recognized.

It was the first record he had ever bought me.

It was most likely given to me as a reward for keeping quiet!

It was a recording of Daniel Barenboim playing three Beethoven sonatas.

The Moonlight, the Appassionata, and the Pathetique.

The cover photo was a portrait of the pianist looking very Beethovian, on an amber background

In the corner, in Jim's handwriting, were the words 'For Charlie'.

I put it on the turntable and turned up the volume.

When Jim had bought me this record I would only have been able to play one handed.

Now, though, I could play these three sonatas fluently.

I'd forgotten how much this record had influenced my playing.

I went back to painting, occasionally sipping scotch.

When the album was finished I put the paint away until tomorrow and went back to the tattoo parlour.

The tattooist was just finishing a broken heart tattoo on the arm of a stout young man.

He rubbed off excess blood and smothered his artwork in Vaseline, then dressed it in gauze to protect it from infection.

"Any problems come back and see me" he said.

The stout young man put his shirt back on and paid the tattooist with a handful of notes.

Now it was my turn.

My tattooist took the drawing and put it in his 'light-box'. Essentially this would enlarge and copy the drawing onto tracing paper.

The tracing paper could then be transferred onto my back. Then the tattooing could begin.

I took my top off and lay, stomach down, on his bench. It was upholstered in blue and was comfortable.

"The gent that had this done before had a hairy back" he told me, but I already knew that. "I have to shave your back too, even though your back's not so hairy".

I guess this is how tattooists do their job.

"I think he was my dad" I told him.

"Who? The hairy bloke?"

"Yes. I think he was my dad".

"Ah" he said, as the penny dropped. "So that's where you got the sketch?"

"I found it in his belongings" I explained.

"Is he dead?" I'm sorry mate" he said.

"He died, not long after the tattoo I think".

"That's a shame. He was a jolly soul. He talked about you, as I recall" he told me.

"Really? I hadn't seen him in years. I've been away".

"Oh yeah. He was proud of you, unless he had another son".

He thought for a minute while he rubbed my back in disinfectant.

"Charlie" he said suddenly. "Is THAT your name?"

"I can't believe it" I said. "Yes, I'm Charlie".

"Well, what do you know!" he exclaimed.

"It's hard to believe" I said.

"Now let me try to remember. Was his name Jim?"

"Yes it was" I confirmed.

"Well Charlie, this will be a proper tribute to your dad, God rest his soul".

"Did he tell you anything about this tattoo? I only just found it" I told him.

The tattooist was transferring the design from the tracing paper onto my back.

"He DID, as I recall. The tree here is the Tree of Life, and the dog is God. Get it? Dog is God spelled backwards!" he said.

"Did he mention anything else?"

"He mentioned a lot of things Charlie. I had him sat here, where you're sat, for three days straight, like you're gonna be!" he said.

"The last time I saw him was about four or five years ago" I told my tattooist.

"Well maybe this will be a way for you to get reacquainted with your dad then!" he said, and I could hear a smile in his voice as he spoke.

He started the tattoo.

It was painful, but nothing I couldn't cope with.

"Is it okay? Not too painful?" he asked me.

"It's fine" I said.

"It gets a bit too much after a few hours, so we'll take a break then" he explained to me.

My tattooist introduced himself as Buck, short for Buckley.

"Hi Buck, good to meet you" I said.

"You too Charlie. I can't say that I'm going to be able to remember a lot of what your dad said. It was a few months ago now" he told me.

"That's okay. I don't expect you to".

"I'll tell you if I remember anything" he said.

"Thanks Buck. I'd appreciate that".

"I reckon this is going to be one fine piece of ink when I'm done" he said.

I told Buck that this was a design I kept seeing.

First on a knife I found, lying in the dirt.

Then on a pendant hanging from a madwoman's neck.

"Mm" said Buck. "I don't know what to tell you mate".

"Maybe it means nothing. Just a coincidence!"

"I personally don't believe in coincidence. But I have a psychic friend, Jenny, who knows all about the Tree of Life. I could show her the sketch if you'd let me have it. I can give it back to you tomorrow".

I didn't know what a psychic could say that might clarify things for me. But I figured it couldn't do any harm.

"Sure" I said. "Show Jenny the sketch. But I really WOULD like it back."

"No problem Charlie".

After a while the needle gun became something I couldn't ignore anymore.

"It's time we took a break anyway" Buck told me.

He wiped his work, smothered it in Vaseline, as I'd seen him do before. Then he dressed it.

I was to keep the tattoo away from water long enough for it to heal, he told me.

I guessed, by that, he was telling me I wouldn't be bathing for a while.

"If you're at a loose end tonight there's a bar I go to. Called the Nightingale, just off the lanes. There's usually a band playing. Jenny will be there" he told me.

"I might do that" I said.

I was in a new town and didn't know anyone.

Why shouldn't I go?

This is how I found myself in a Brighton bar on a summer evening.

Buck spotted me at the bar and waved me over to his table.
Buck was soon introducing me to his red-headed, curly
haired companion, Jenny.
I recognized her.
She was the centrefold model in Jim's Penthouse
magazine.
This was Eugenie.
I decided that the best course of action would be for me
not to let her know that I recognized her.
I was sure it would only appear tacky if I was to do that.
If the subject arose then maybe I could mention that I'd
seen her work.
She was dressed in an emerald green summer dress.
She must have chosen the colour especially because it
matched her eyes so well.
Her full lips were shaped for smiling, even when at rest.
"This is my psychic friend" Buck said.
"How does THAT work?" I asked her.
"Only sometimes" she admitted. "I don't tell the future so
much as 'read' people".
"I bet THAT comes in handy" I said to her.
"Charlie is in the middle of getting a tattoo done" Buck
informed her. "It's going to be pretty impressive when it's
finished".
"What are you having done?" she asked me.
"Wait" said Buck. "Can I show Jenny the drawing?"
"Of course" I said.
He unfolded the picture and she assessed it quietly for a
moment.
"The Tree of Life" she confirmed. "You can see the ten
spheres of the tree quite distinctly all the way from
Malkuth to Kether."
"That's all Greek to me" I told her.

"It's Hebrew" she corrected.

"And what does it mean?" I asked.

She laughed heartily.

"Scholars spend years, decades, studying the Tree, and you want me to explain it in a sentence" she shook her head.

"Can you give him the gist?" asked Buck.

Jenny sighed.

"I can try" she began. "It symbolises all the forces in the universe, the ten spheres are the different forces."

"I hope it's a GOOD symbol and not some satanic tattoo I'm getting!" I queried.

"Oh, it's a great symbol of protection" she told me.

I was relieved at the news.

"What about the dog?" Buck asked her.

"Well, the dog isn't something you'd usually see on the Tree, but it looks to me like it's guarding the Gates of Hell keeping the demons locked in" she was happy to inform me.

Buck told Jenny that this was a symbol I'd been seeing everywhere.

"How strange!" she said.

"I thought you might be able to enlighten him" said Buck, "you being the psychic and all."

She was quick to laugh.

"I keep telling you Buck, I prefer to be called a Sensitive!" Then she explained. "It's the same thing really, but people are uncomfortable around psychics, happy to shoot them down in flames, together with their beliefs".

Buck, as you'd imagine, had tattoos on both arms. I was in no doubt that the rest of his body was equally as covered. The tattoos that were visible, right up to the sleeves of his T-shirt were of every description and style, and of varying quality.

Seeing Buck's tattoos I was reminded why we were having this conversation.

I told Jenny about my father. I explained that I hadn't seen him for years and that he had recently died. I told her that I was soon to be wearing what had been his last tattoo.

"I think that's wonderful" she said.

I let her think that. I certainly wasn't going to explain the many extreme emotions that his memory stirred up in me.

"I can give you a reading if you'd like" she offered.

I wasn't sure what this entailed.

She brought a Tarot pack out of her big damask bag.

She asked me to shuffle, which I did.

She asked me to pull a card out from anywhere in the middle of the pack.

I handed it to her.

It was the Magician.

She asked for another card.

It was the Fool.

"One more" she said.

I pulled out the Death card.

Jenny was very quick to point out that Death didn't *always* mean 'death'.

"It probably *does* mean your father's death in this case though" she explained.

"So what does it mean?" I asked her, intrigued now.

"I don't want you to think I can see the future, but sometimes the things I say DO come true. I just want to tell you that right from the start" she told me.

She closed her eyes and took a breath.

Then she was ready to continue.

She opened her eyes.

The room seemed to go quiet around me as I listened to her.

Of course this was just my imagination.

I'm sure I was just focussed on Jenny to the exclusion of all else.

"These forces are all very strong in you at the moment. You are both the Magician and the Fool even though Death seems to be all around you. The Fool tells me that you are innocent, and the Innocent are greatly protected, even when under the fiercest attack. The Magician tells me that you express yourself through a great gift. Is that music?" she asked, but didn't wait for a reply.

"You've suffered greatly, and always blamed yourself, even though you were blameless. Every single sign that you see around you is there to be interpreted. They've been placed there for your protection. Nevertheless, your safety depends on how you interpret those signs."

Jenny had me enthralled by her reading.

I was aware of her scent.

Patchouli.

It was intoxicating.

"Very soon everything will become clear to you. Some things have already shown themselves to you, but you still don't have the full picture".

She paused to look at me.

"Aside from that, Charlie, it seems that the worst is over" and she smiled, her whole face lighting up.

It seemed that my reading was over.

"She's good, isn't she?" said Buck.

"Oh yes" I agreed.

"Anyway, the band is about to start" he added.

Any conversation after this point was either shouted or in sign language, or a happy mixture of the two.

The night wore on in a joyous cacophony of loud music, shouting and laughter.

I got more and more drunk, but happily so.
I said my goodbyes at the end of the night.
I made it back 'home' and threw myself onto my stepfather's bed.
The next day I painted, while listening to Beethoven.
Then I had another third of my Tree tattooed on my back.
Later still I went to the Nightingale and met Buck and Jenny.
The conversation was light, unlike the previous evening.
A different band played, called Caught In The Act.
The guitarist was among the most talented I had ever heard.
Jenny wasn't in the best of moods.
I asked her why.
She told me her car, a Mini, had died on her. It was only good for scrap now.
I was drunk enough to make a grand gesture.
"You want a car?" I asked her. "I have a car!"
I told her about the red Jaguar.
"Oh Charlie, don't be silly! I couldn't take your Jag off you" she said, but I could read in her eyes that she half hoped I would let her have it.
I insisted. I don't know why. I was drunk.
"It probably needs some work" I told her, and then explained, "My father was working on it when he died".
"Oh then I definitely couldn't accept it!" she exclaimed, and the disappointment was clear on her face.
"Why? Because it might need some work?" I asked her.
"No, of course not. Because it was your father's!"
Our night was quickly at an end, and there was an invitation for me to come for the third night.
The last day was almost an exact replica of the previous days.

I painted and then Buck finished my tattoo.

He made me stand between two full length mirrors so I could see it in its full glory.

It was, and still is, magnificent.

I paid Buck for his work and promised to meet up later.

I had something to do back at the bungalow before heading to the Nightingale.

My back was very sore and I was my head was aching a bit from so much ale, the night before, (and the night before that too).

I found a public phone and called Doc briefly, just to make sure everything was okay at home.

It was all fine, he said.

Scout was missing me.

He was missing me too.

I told him how much I loved him, but said nothing about my new tattoo.

I didn't want to worry him, or make him think I was losing my mind.

There was nothing to worry about anyway.

I certainly wasn't in danger of losing my mind.

The Nightingale beckoned.

Jenny and Buck were already there.

They smiled a huge welcome.

"I need you to do a bit of paperwork" I told Jenny.

She looked at me as if I was Drugs Squad.

"Relax" I told her. "I want to sign the Jag over to you".

I'd filled out MY part of the log-book, and now it was HER turn.

"Now, don't argue with me" I warned her.

I'm sure there were tears beginning to form at the corner of her eyes, but she filled out the form anyway.

The form could now be pulled in two at the centre, where it was serrated.

I had a stamped and addressed envelope ready to send to the Licensing Office.

Once I had both parts of the form I placed them both in the envelope, sealed it, and left the pub to find the nearest post box.

Without hesitation I dropped the envelope in the box and rejoined Buck and Jenny.

"That was a good thing you did there mate" Buck said to me.

"Just trying to keep one step ahead of Karma" I told him.

The jaguar would only have been worth a couple of hundred pounds, and I had more money in my account than I knew what to do with.

I also had a property that would bring me in a healthy monthly amount.

I felt I could afford to be generous.

Very soon a band started to play.

This was a different band, called Emptifish.

The lead singer was a charismatic and bald man with thick glasses. The band members all wore suits. It was quite a show.

The audience went wild for them.

As usual I drank far too much.

I danced and then drank some more.

At the end of the night we all swapped details; phone numbers and addresses.

We promised to keep in touch.

I thought they were a magical couple.

We said our goodbyes.

Jenny's goodbye was especially warm.

She pressed her full lips to mine and then pulled me close to her.

"Ouch!" I winced.

"Careful Jenny" said Buck. "Charlie's tattoo!"

"Sorry" she said, and let me go.

I made my way home, hoping with every step that I'd meet Buck and Jenny again.

I was deeply sad to say goodbye to them.

The next day I flew from Gatwick to Dublin.

I hired a car and drove to County Down, which was now a familiar route.

I reached Newry and booked myself into the Canal Court Hotel.

From there I went to the police station to let them know I was available for further questioning.

It was strange going back to the police station.

I had a feeling that I would be whisked into an interview room, given a blood test and fingerprinted, like before.

Then I'd be thrown into a holding cell to await Behan's pleasure.

I told the policeman at the reception desk that I was staying at the Canal Court Hotel.

He told me he'd let Behan know.

I have to say this. I described it as a reception desk, but in those days Newry police station would have been a very secure building, and the reception desk was a reinforced booth behind bullet proof glass. These were the years of 'The Troubles'.

I went back to the hotel, shaved, showered, (trying not to let water get onto my new tattoo), and then watched some television in my room.

The phone rang.

I was expecting the call to be from Behan.

I was surprised when the hotel's telephone receptionist told me that Mr Mick O'Brien wanted to speak to me.

"Mr Watson?" he asked.

"Yes! how did you know I was here?"

"I'm an investigative reporter Mr Watson. That's what I do" he explained.

"I'm sorry" I told him. "My situation hasn't changed. I'm still not at liberty to talk about the incident. I still need to talk to the police".

"I understand that Mr Wilson" he said. "I'm not calling because I want to ASK you something." He let that hang in the air for a second.

"I want us to meet up because I want to TELL you something".

I was intrigued now.

I was prepared to meet, I said, just as long as our meeting didn't jeopardise my dealings with the police.

He promised me.

I believed his promise.

We arranged to meet in ten minutes time, in the bar downstairs.

I thought I had enough time to call Doc, just to let him know I'd arrived safely.

He picked up after three or so rings.

"Hello?" I heard his familiar voice.

"Doc, it's me. I thought I'd let you know I arrived safe."

"That's good. Any news?" he asked.

"I got a call from that reporter. He wants to meet. Says he has something for me, news relating to the case" I said.

Doc was breathing heavily now.

"Don't trust him" he said. "Don't trust anyone!"

"I'll be fine Doc. The police know I'm here at the hotel. I just want this all behind us. How's Roger, and Scout?" I asked.

Everyone's fine here" he said. "I just want you to be very careful" he said.

There was something about Doc's tone.

I felt the familiar feeling in my stomach.

The feeling of dread.

"I'll be careful" I told him. "I promise".

"I love you Charlie" he said.

"Love you too Doc" I said, and put the phone down.

O'Brien was already waiting for me at the bar and rose to meet me.

"You must be Charlie Watson" he said.

"And you must be Mick O'Brien".

"Get you a drink?"

I chose a glass of lager.

He got us our drinks and we sat at a table. It was early enough that no one else, aside from the barman, was in the place.

"What did you want to tell me?" I asked him.

"Well first I just wanted to get some things straight. Don't worry. I'm keeping my promise. This doesn't jeopardise anything with the police."

"Okay" I said. "Shoot".

"I just need to confirm this. Was your travel companion Doctor Des Farnham?" he asked.

"What does this have to do with him?" I asked.

"That's difficult to answer unless you answer my question first" he explained.

I thought about it.

"Okay" I agreed. "Des Farnham was my companion".
"How long have you been living together?" he asked.
Instinctively I answered "That's none of your business".
He knew from my answer that Doc and I HAD been living
together, probably for a while.
"Look, Doc and I are lovers" I admitted. "I can't see how
any of that is going to be of interest to your readers."
I got up to leave.
"Mr Watson, wait" O'Brien said. "Calls were made from
your home phone! A home you share with Farnham"
I didn't know what he could be talking about.
"I have my sources, which obviously I can't reveal" he
said. "For the minute I just want you to trust me on this
and listen to everything I'm about to say".
"Firstly, the police have completely cleared you, by all
accounts. The forensic results are beyond question. If I
give you all the information that I have then all I want in
return is a story from you, when you're ready to give it. I'd
say THAT story, the one you'll give me, would be of
interest to my readers" he said.
I sat back down again.
"What do you mean, that calls were made from my home
phone?"
"Let me just clarify for you. I'm not talking about YOUR
phone. I'm talking about the phone that is in Farnham's
name" he said.
"What about it?" I asked.
"The police got a hold of the phone records. It was
discovered that calls were made from Farnham's phone to
Liam Coleman weeks before your trip to Ireland. What do
you make of that?" he asked.
I honestly couldn't make head nor tail of it.
It made no sense.

I knew that Doc had been calling his Aunt Mary.
Could that be where the confusion lay?
"No," said O'Brien. "Someone, using Farnham's phone, called Coleman's phone."
I thought long and hard about this.
O'Brien could see me trying to join the dots.
He decided to help.
"If YOU didn't call Coleman, then someone else DID. That someone HAD to be Farnham. You have to ask yourself, why did Farnham call Liam Coleman? What was that call about?"
"No" I said. "Doc didn't know Coleman".
"I'm afraid there's more, Mr Watson" he added.
"The police got Farnham's bank records and it seems that he withdrew a substantial amount, in sterling, just before your trip".
"Well of course" I said. "We needed sterling for our holiday".
"The amount that was withdrawn was just over three thousand pounds" he said. "which is almost the same amount of money found in Coleman's sports bag".
I thought for a minute.
I decided that it had to be coincidence, and told O'Brien what I thought.
"Is it coincidence that Farnham's prints were found on the money in the sports bag?" he asked me. "How do you explain that?"
Of course this all had to be a huge mistake.
And anyway, why would Doc be giving money to Liam Coleman?
None of it made sense.
"How did you get Farnham's prints?" I asked. I was conscious that I'd stopped referring to him as Doc.

"I would have been instrumental in obtaining Farnham's prints, Mr Watson. Farnham is Irish by birth but gave his fingerprints when he applied for new citizenship. He was also arrested in his youth, and his prints taken then. They're on record. But don't worry about that for now".

It sounded like a huge invasion of privacy as far as I was concerned, and I didn't think anything would stand up in court. And what, exactly, was O'Brien accusing Doc of doing? Doc wasn't a murderer or coke dealer.

"I'm going to give you time to put all the pieces together, and when you're ready you can call me on this number" he said, handing me his card.

He swigged down the last of his drink, and then left me alone in the hotel bar so I could think about what he said.

Not long after that I got a call from Behan.

He asked me to visit him in the police station, informally, (he stressed).

I'm sure that if I had preferred another venue then he would have agreed.

As it was I had no problem meeting him in the police station.

He shook my hand when we met, and I knew then that he had no intention of arresting me.

I was completely innocent in the whole proceedings, and forensics had proved it.

The butterflies in my stomach were a different thing.

It was the familiar feeling of dread.

Behan led me to the same interview room I'd been in before.

We went through the events of that night, one more time.

Behan was satisfied with that.

Then he started to bring up the things that O'Brien had just told me.

The phone records, the money withdrawals, the fingerprints.

This implied that what O'Brien had told me was true.

It also meant that nothing Behan said could take me by surprise.

Behan noticed this.

"None of this seems to surprise you Mr Watson. Why's that?" he asked.

"I've just had a conversation with Mr O'Brien from the Newry Reporter" I admitted.

Behan looked serious.

"And after I suggested to you that you NOT talk to the press?" he said.

I stressed to Behan that I didn't reveal anything, and that it was O'Brien who revealed everything.

Anyway, Behan had only SUGGESTED I not talk to the police. It wasn't an order.

"We're presented with a puzzle" said Behan. "Farnham hands three thousand pounds to Coleman. We know, from your statement, that they were in the house at the same time."

I remembered that they really HAD been in the house at the same time, if only for a minute.

"The question is WHY?" he asked. "Can you think of anything?"

I told him I couldn't.

"The problem we have is that there's evidence that links Farnham and Coleman but that proves nothing. There's no crime here that I can see. Unless you can shed a light on things?" he asked me.

I told him I couldn't.

He scrutinised me to see if I was lying.
He must have had years of experience, telling truth from lies, and he nodded at me finally. I had told the truth and he knew it.
I felt there was something I wasn't seeing.
I asked Behan if he was telling me everything.
He told me he was.
"Is there anything else you can think of?" he asked me.
The only thing I thought might be useful was that Doc's Aunty Mary had apparently taken the booking for the guest house from Coleman.
Maybe that could be a lead.
Behan let me go.
Unless I could think of something he didn't need me anymore.
I was free to leave the country.
Which is what I did.
On the next flight the following day.

I handed the car keys back to the car hire firm at Dublin airport.
I checked in and made it to the bar.
I ordered a Guinness and popped a Valium.
I tried to put everything in an order.
Doc had been in touch with Jim Fox/Liam Coleman long before we went to Ireland.
Doc handed over three thousand pounds which was found in the sports bag.
To my way of thinking it seemed obvious that Doc was paying Jim/Liam to do something, but what?
What tied it all together?
I couldn't figure it all out.

I guessed the only thing to do was ask Doc when I next saw him.

The flight would land in eight hours.

I would see Doc in nine hours or so.

I'd see Scout and Roger too.

I might be able to figure it all out by myself in that time.

I was certain there was a feasible explanation for everything.

The feeling of dread overtook me for a second when I thought that maybe I'd imagined the whole thing.

Had I imagined Jim Fox, Brian, Anto, Behan, O'Brien and even Aunty Mary and cousin Agnes?

The Guinness and Valium sent me down a whirlpool of doubt and I had to take a deep breath.

I looked at all the people, all the events, and all the evidence.

I knew they were all real.

That wasn't the problem.

There was something I was missing, that was all.

One final piece and the puzzle would make sense.

I wondered if I should call Doc from the public phone.

I'd leave it for now.

I realized that, if it was noon here in Dublin, it was four in the morning back at home.

Chapter Eight

By the time the cab pulled up outside the house it was two in the afternoon, local time.

Roger was home but Doc wasn't.

Roger was wearing his waiter's uniform of white shirt and black trousers.

He had yet don his clip-on bow-tie.
"I need to talk to you Charlie" he said.
"Well I need to talk to you too Roger" I told him.
Scout wouldn't leave my side.
"Is Doc giving his lectures?" I asked.
Roger nodded.
"It's Doc I need to speak to you about" he said. "It's driving me crazy".
"Well I need to speak to you about Doc too" I said.
I wondered if we might both be speaking about the same thing.
Roger rolled a joint as if the act of rolling might clear his mind.
It was like a meditation technique.
He began to talk.
"Nick's a good kid" he said, as if that was connected to what he was saying.
"Yeah" I agreed. "A bit quiet though. I'd be happier if he was running around like a mad thing."
"Maybe there's a reason for that!" Roger was hinting at something.
"For Christ's sake spit it out Roger" I said. "What's going on?"
"Nick started to say something to me, almost by accident, and then, as soon as he said it, he shut up" Roger said.
"What on earth could he have said?"
"I'm not sure of anything Charlie. I don't want to be accusing anyone of anything. There's probably nothing going on. I could be making mountains out of molehills" he said.
He passed the joint to me.
"Listen Roger, I'm pretty certain Doc isn't abusing his own kid. Was that what you were trying to say?" I asked him.

I wasn't annoyed.

I just thought Roger had the wrong end of the stick.

Roger remained silent.

I had a sudden thought.

"I just have to go upstairs" I said.

I took my rucksack up to the bedroom I shared with Doc, dumped the rucksack, and the retrieved my knife from the drawer.

I took it back downstairs with me.

I hadn't shown it to Roger before but I showed it to him now.

"Very nice" he said.

The look on his face told me he didn't quite get what I was trying to say.

"Have a closer look at the markings" I told him.

"Cool design" he said.

"I went a bit wild when I was away" I grinned.

I took off my shirt and showed him my back.

"Oh man!" he exclaimed.

"It still needs to heal a bit" I told him. "I had it done while I was in England".

"It's beautiful Charlie" he said, "but I don't get it. You're not exactly the biker type!"

I did my best to explain how I acquired my tattoo.

I pulled the sketch from my wallet, unfolded it, and showed it to Roger.

"No" he said. "I still don't get it!"

I told him to compare the carving on the knife with the tattoo, and the sketch.

"They all seem identical" he agreed.

He handed me the knife.

I held the knife in my hand for a second.

"Do you know what Roger? I'm done with knives" and I handed it back to him.

"You're giving it to me?" he asked.

I nodded.

He slipped the knife into his black waiter's trousers.

"Did I ever tell you about Doc's cousin, Agnes?" I asked him.

He shook his head.

It seemed that, within the more dramatic story, Agnes had been lost.

Roger had always assumed that the wound in my hand had been caused by Jim/Liam.

It was already such a complicated story that mention of Agnes and her dementia would have made it even more incomprehensible.

Roger had only been given the edited version of events until now.

"So what does this have to do with your tattoo?" he asked me.

"Agnes had this same design on a pendant around her neck" I explained.

Roger shrugged.

He still didn't get it.

I reminded him about the day that I found Duffy's broken body at the foot of a tree.

"Well" he admitted. "I can definitely see a black dog at the foot of a tree!"

So I told Roger how Scout had found the knife at the foot of the same tree, or at least guided me to it.

"Now it's just getting spooky Charlie" he said.

"That's what I'm talking about Roger! It IS fucking spooky! I don't know what to make of it".

Roger shook his head at me, grinning from ear to ear.

"And your solution is to get a 'fuck off' tattoo on your back? Way to go!" he laughed.

I guess it was all in Roger's delivery, because I laughed too.

Roger rolled another joint and I got us both another beer.

I knew I'd have to practice piano soon. I'd been away from it too long.

I could put it off for another little while.

"I have to go to work tonight anyway" said Roger. "You can practice then".

He lit up the joint.

Mick's plant had served us well but there were now only a few smokes left.

I told Roger about my meeting with O'Brien, and then the one with Behan.

I told Roger about the phone calls and the three thousand pounds.

"Oh God Charlie!" Roger said. "Doc put a contract out on you!"

"Fuck off!" I said. "Why would Doc do such a thing? He loves me".

"He does now you've got all this money!" he argued.

"No" I was adamant. "There's another explanation".

"Then you're just going to have to ask him, aren't you?"

"Anyway" I told him. "I think I have it figured out".

"Okay Sherlock" he said. "Tell me".

"Aunt Mary must have told Doc that other guests would be arriving on the same day as us. Doc must have told her to cancel, but she gave Doc the phone number so HE could get them to cancel".

"Mm, okay. That works" agreed Roger. "It explains the phone call".

He passed me the joint.

"But that doesn't explain the money" he added.

"Simple!" I explained. "Doc drew out the extra money for the trip, and it was in our room. Coleman must have gone into our room when I was taking a bath and stolen the money!"

Roger thought it through.

"Case solved" he said.

My grin wasn't on my lips for long.

Although it was AN explanation, it still might not be THE explanation.

I still needed to talk to Doc.

But I didn't feel so bad now.

Roger was putting his jacket on over his waiter's uniform. The phone rang.

"Hi Doc. Where are you?" I said into the receiver.

It wasn't Doc.

"Mr Watson?" said the voice, which I recognized as that of Behan from the Newry Police.

"Speaking" I answered.

After an unnecessary introduction he told me he'd been speaking to Doc.

"I was able to reach him at the university" he elaborated.

"I just finished speaking to him. I questioned him regarding those loose ends we discussed, and I'm afraid to tell you that his response was unsatisfactory" he said, but I cut across him.

"It's okay, I figured out what must have happened" I said, and began to give my explanation.

Roger was about to leave, but I signalled him to stay for a second.

"That's all well and good Mr Watson. In fact it would explain everything. The only problem is that Doctor Farnham was unable to give me any such explanation" he paused. "The reason I'm calling you is because I wanted to make you aware that Farnham now knows that YOU know. About the money, about the fingerprints, and about the phone records. About his general involvement in the events we've been investigating" he explained.

"Well, I was going to chat with him about all that anyway, just as soon as he gets back" I said.

"No Mr Watson. I'm trying to tell you that I'm actually very concerned for your safety."

He let that sink in for a second.

"Well thank you very much Mr Behan" I said.

"Detective Inspector" he corrected.

"Well thank you very much Detective Inspector Behan, I appreciate your concerns for my safety but I'm certain Doctor Farnham will make everything clear once he gets home".

Behan tried to speak again but I cut him short.

"Goodbye Detective Inspector Behan" I said and put the phone down.

"That sounded intense" said Roger.

"Mm. Listen I should let you get to work" I said. "We can catch up later".

"Do you fancy the Tower tonight?" he asked.

"I'll see" I answered.

Although I would still pay the odd visit to the Tower, it wasn't a place that Doc would frequent.

"Fine. Smell ya later" he said, and he was gone.

I was alone.

First I took Scout for a quick walk.

I'd missed my puppy.

When I got home with Scout I went to the grand piano and started to play the Kabalevsky.

My left hand had healed very well and the first chord was no longer the painful stretch that it used to be.

I was absorbed in the piece now.

The front door burst open and it crashed noisily against the wall.

I stopped playing.

"What the fuck have you been saying about me?" screamed a voice I recognized as Doc's.

I turned round on the piano stool.

Doc was wide eyed, looking both scared and angry.

In his hand he held a gun I didn't know he possessed.

He was aiming it at me now.

'So this is how it ends' I thought.

The blindfold suddenly fell away from me, completely, once and for all.

I was calm.

If this was how it was going to end then I was ready.

Roger had been right.

Doc had needed money and he'd put a contract out on me.

He'd handed Jim Fox the money as he left our bedroom that night.

I remembered now.

Doc had been carrying a toiletry bag, only it contained three thousand pounds, not toiletries.

There were other memories now.

Jim Fox had said something like 'you were supposed to be lying dead here, not Anto and Brian'.

Jim Fox had just let everything get out of control because of his coke fuelled frenzy.

If not for that then I would have been lying dead in my bed.

I thought of the photo that Doc had acquired from my mother.

Yes, it was a picture of my stepfather.

It was also a pretty good picture of ME; skinny and younger, but still ME!

Was it the same photo that Brian burned, and then lit his cigarette from it?

Had Doc given Jim the photo so as to identify me as the contract, the hit?

I remembered how Doc had tried to get back up to the guest house that night.

I realized, only now, that he had wanted to erase any evidence of his involvement.

All these thoughts and memories flashed through my mind in an instant.

Doc was still pointing the gun at me and still had mad, angry eyes.

"Was it all just about money Doc?" I asked.

I KNEW that it was all about the money, and must have been right from the minute I signed the insurance policy.

I don't know WHAT it had all been about up till then. I thought it had been love! I was being played.

Doc was screaming at me again.

"Why did you have to fuck with it? We were all right. We could have moved on. Forgotten all about Coleman's fuck up. We HAVE money now!"

I sat calmly at the piano, but Doc was getting closer.

My heart was breaking, but I was still calm.

"I can still make this work" he snarled at me. "Get up. You're coming with me".

I shook my head.

"I'm going nowhere Doc. This is my house. If you want to kill me you'll have to do it here."

I couldn't believe what I was saying.

"What about Nick?" I said.

"What about him?" he hissed. "This was all for HIM."
Then it occurred to me that Roger might have hit on
something earlier.
I was going to say something like 'you don't want your kid
to grow up with a father in prison', or something similar.
Something, anything to get me out of this fix.
I didn't say that.
"Have you been sexually abusing your own kid Doc? Your
own fucking kid?" I said instead.
"You nasty minded little cunt" Doc screeched at me.
He fired a shot.
It burned my side, such a pain as I never felt before.
The blood was gushing out of the wound.
I was swaying about on the piano stool now, first
threatening to fall back, then forward.
I fell back, onto the piano keys.
The piano made a dissonant squawk.
I was at Doc's mercy now more than ever.
I was feeling dizzy.
I was seeing the dead submariners dancing together
underwater, wearing their black and white uniforms.
I knew I was soon going to join them.
One of the submariners had pulled a knife.
All the other ghostly submariners seemed to swim
together, converging on the one with the knife. They
became one submariner.
Only it wasn't one submariner.
It was a waiter in his black and white uniform.
It was Roger, and he had wrestled Doc to the floor and had
stabbed him.
The room seemed to strobe; from yellow to black, like a
wasp.
Two policeman were at the broken front door.

They pulled Roger away from Doc.
Then they confiscated the gun, and the knife.
That was the last I saw of anything.
I had lost consciousness.

I regained consciousness a little while later, in the ambulance.
My wound was being dressed by one of the crew.
"You'll live. Just a flesh wound" he said. "Could have been nasty though".
The bullet had miraculously missed my vital organs.

I was made to stay overnight.
Al and Rob visited me the next morning.
"Who's looking after Scout?" was all I could think of to say.
"We have Scout, don't worry" Al told me, but I was already drifting off again.

When I came to, it was probably only minutes later.
Rob and Al were still there, but a police officer was with them.
He asked them to leave the room.
The officer asked me for a brief statement.
My words seemed to confirm what he already knew.
He told me that Roger and Doc had been held for questioning.
He said that Detective Inspector Behan had called my local police station the minute that I'd hung up on him.
Behan's call had instigated a police visit, which had arrived just in time to pull Roger from Doc.
Behan had filled in all the missing pieces of the puzzle.
Roger was free to go, but Doc would be detained.

I felt euphoric, and figured that some of my euphoria
might be because of the morphine I'd been given.
I was reminded of Mrs Van Nord.
With her memory came the smell of lavender.
The officer left.
Al and Rob were back.
Roger was with them.
He was going to take me home just as soon as I was ready.
The staff said I'd be ready to leave by the next day.
A male nurse poked his head into the room.
"Your parents are here to visit you" he said. "I'm afraid
you're only allowed three visitors at a time though".
"It's okay" said Roger. "We'll leave you to it".
I wasn't in a fit state to argue.
I really believe that if it hadn't been for the morphine I
would have been able to handle anything.
Unfortunately, the nature of morphine is that it makes you
lose your grip of reality.
Riff and my mother entered the room.
Riff had a gift of some grapes.
My mother helped herself to them as she spoke.
"I can't believe the professor would shoot you" she was
telling me.
Riff knew well enough to stay in the background now.
He'd made his encouraging noises and he'd brought grapes.
"You must have done something to antagonize him!" she
said sternly.
I couldn't believe what she was saying.
No, I lie.
I believed she was saying it.
It's just the way she is.
I had a trick up my sleeve.
"Oh I meant to tell you" I said matter-of-factly" I said.

"Yes dear" she said sweetly.

"That letter, the one you gave me" I waited until I could see she remembered.

"Oh yes dear. Who was it from?" She was smiling at me like a queen of great beneficence.

"It was Jim Watson's solicitor".

She frowned slightly.

"Yes! He said that Jim Watson's dead". I sounded as nonchalant as the day she'd told me about Mrs Van Nord's death. I let the information sink in.

"How terrible" she said.

"Indeed. He left me everything; a house, a small fortune, and a car". She didn't need to know that I'd already made a gift of the car.

My mother was suddenly very angry.

"Well that's ridiculous. By rights that should all be mine. After all I put up with. And to give it to you! You're nothing more than an ungrateful little shit!" she ranted.

"You're quite right mother" I said, letting the morphine wash over me. "I'll tell you what though. Have a word with handsome Peter Van Nord; see if you can get me back the piano you promised me. Then I'll let you have Jim Watson's money. And the house".

I could see that Riff was suppressing laughter.

"Well, I can have a word with Peter, of course. I doubt that he owns the piano anymore. I would say he's sold it."

She had no idea I was playing her.

"Oh well, never mind" I said.

Riff suggested that they leave so I could get some rest.

I drifted away on a morphine cloud.

I dreamed.

I was on a mountainside.

There was a yellow car.
Inside the yellow car were some dogs, among them Duffy,
They howled hysterically.
A hooded man, bearing a huge axe, was swinging at the
rear window.
He was incredibly and impossibly muscled, and the sweat
glistened on his magnificent torso and arms.
I could hear the incongruous ringing of a telephone.
The ringing pulled me back into wakefulness.
I answered the phone.
"Hello dear" came my mother's voice.

Chapter Nine

I keep a diary, meticulously.
Without it I would lose track of my days.
I have no doubt I would also forget any dream that the
nights might visit upon me.
Without a diary I might not even be able to tell them apart.

I was wide awake, and busily writing the entry for Friday
the first of February.
I described as much of my dream as I could, in as much
detail.
Thanks to my diary of 1980 I'm able to fill in any and all
of the gaps in my dream.

I was almost sure my dream had been a premonition.
I'd told my mother to look after the dogs, especially Duffy.
She promised me that she would, and that they'd be safe
because the dog-run was so secure.
She collected me at the end of my school day.

She would normally be in the habit of stopping at a gas station and filling the tank of her yellow car. She had made such a stop in my vivid dream of last night.

I had looked at the gauge and seen that the quarter tank would be more than enough to get us home to River House.

We might save valuable minutes.

I knew that we'd see Annabel out on the road, and that there would be three snotty-nosed boys on the dry-stone wall.

What use is a premonition, I thought, if it changes nothing?

I persuaded my mother NOT to stop off at the gas station.

I'd persuaded her to drive just a little faster than she otherwise would have.

We saw Annabel in the road, as I'd dreamed.

"Drive on" I ordered her, and there must have been something in my tone that made her obey.

My mother is not the kind of woman to obey anyone, least of all ME!

We turned the corner, and THERE walking towards River House were three boys, all aged about ten.

And THERE, about to cross the road, was Duffy.

I leapt from the car and grabbed him by his collar, just as an enormous ten-wheeled truck drove over the spot Duffy WOULD have just crossed.

Annabel made it home safely, about half an hour later.

"You KNEW that was going to happen" said my mother.
I shrugged.

Nothing else from my dream came true, at least not in the way I dreamed it.

There was no knife under the tree.
Doc and I never became lovers.
It all seemed to hinge on saving Duffy.
I was quite happy with that!
Duffy, my most favourite dog in the world.
He went on to live for another five years.
His muzzle grew more grey with each Summer.
He grew stiffer with each Winter.
He eventually found movement so painful and difficult
that it seemed best to put him to sleep.
I held him in my arms, telling him he was a good boy and
how much I loved him, as the life drained from him.
I knew that I would one day meet him again, if there really
IS a Heaven, and if I'm ever allowed in.

This was still February the first though.
Duffy was alive.
I was working two jobs waiting tables..
I was teaching piano every Saturday.
I played church organ every Sunday.
I practiced the Kabalevsky, every day.
I was beginning to feel that 1980 might just be MY year,
and that the eighties might even be my decade.

Printed in Great Britain
by Amazon

58154398R00154